Terraforming Venus

Illustrated

Tales From an Alternate

Steampunk History

Book 1

2nd Edition

Timothy M Dooley

Terraforming of Venus is based on the first part of a short story called "The Gardner". It is from my Alternate History timeline series and was posted on September 2011. It's a story of a few immortals who helped turn a hostile, hellish world into a second Earth, a new world. Yet, despite humanity's greatest accomplishments and achievements, humanity can also be its own worst nightmare. This book is dedicated to all those who enjoy science fiction and especially to those who remember Jules Verne and are into Steampunk.

Sincerely

Timothy M Dooley

Throughout history there have been stories, legends, and even religions about those who have never tasted death. They are sometimes referred to as gods, angels, demons, or simply immortals. As they walk among us, they share in our life's experiences and dreams. Not knowing their true nature, we interact with them, sometimes for better, sometimes for worse. Like us, their influence shapes history. But unlike us time for them passes much slower as they live through the centuries. As a result, they oversee history's grand events from beginning to end, and often they influence the course of humanity.

1. RONALD POWERS TERRA stood alone on one of the highest places of Avalon Island overlooking the South Atlantic Ocean in the early morning hours. The bright star of Venus dominated the sky.

The rocky ice-covered island he called Avalon had been his secluded home for many years. It was one of the few places on Earth where he felt safe. Less than a hundred miles off the coast of Antarctica, its cold wasteland appearance was of no interest to passing ships. In the early morning hours, Ronald Powers Terra stood alone on one of the highest places of the island overlooking the South Atlantic Ocean. The bright star of Venus dominated the sky. As he looked out at the dark horizon, he thought about all the lives he had lived through the centuries. As far as he knew, he believed he was the first of his kind, the first immortal.

Ronald Powers Terra was the tenth generation of the Terra line. His mind had inhabited nine previous bodies. Like the previous eight (that were re-generated) who lived before him, he was first born at the approximate age of 24 with the full memories of the earlier Terra generations, except the two who were killed before they could pass on their memories. The year was 2273 and at the age of 74, the 50-year life span of his current body was about to come to an end. He would soon go to the Greenhouse and surrender his memories to the next body (or generation). As Terra continued to look out over the dark ocean, he thought about how immortality all started.

The early Terra generations had to live in the shadow of their grandfather "Powers Terra" and his horrifying legacy. He became known as the creator of monsters after events of the first Mars expedition were made public back in 1763. As a result, the Terra's that followed lived their lives in seclusion as they also pursued the art of re-engineering life itself. But unlike their grandfather (or the first one), they were not monsters and hoped all of humanity would benefit from their work.

2. POWERS TERRA was the first human to achieve true immortality.

Powers Terra was born in Oslo Norway in 1706. Unlike the others, he was born of natural birth and lived to be 117. Early in his life he had invented a way to stop ageing when he slept. But in 1823 he wrote in his diary about waking up from his death bed in a younger body that was approximately 24 years old. He wrote of having a dream where a dark stranger in the shadows told him he would have to renew himself in 50 years. The stranger said he would find a way. He changed his name to Edward Powers

Terra, faked the death of Powers Terra, and claimed full inheritance. 1823 marked the beginning of the second Terra generation. From that time on, every 23rd and 73rd year of every century, the Terra generation changed (barring an unexpected event).

3. POWERS TERRA wrote of having a dream where a dark stranger in the shadows told him he would have to renew himself in 50 years. The stranger said he would find a way.

In his second generation, Terra had changed. He no longer had complete disregard of human life in the pursuit of his research. His body had changed. It had become somewhat plant like. His strength had increased and his tolerance of heat and cold was much greater. The Terras that came after Powers worked to conceal their true identity. They often worked quietly as silent partners alongside famous medical researchers, botanists, and others involved in life sciences. They lived mostly in isolation. In later years, Terra was referred to as "The Gardener" by the others he introduced to immortality.

As Ronald Powers Terra continued to think of how it all started, he remembered the advent of immortality began in 1731 when members of a lunar construction crew were investigating the damage of an underground settlement after a massive lunar quake. They accidentally discovered a vast network of caves that stretched all around the Moon. They were also astonished to find that the caves had a breathable atmosphere. When word got out of the discovery, professional cave explorers and map makers descended on the Moon. The air pressure in the caverns was equivalent to that on Earth at an elevation of 7600 feet [2316.5 meters]. The real mystery was wondering where the oxygen was coming from. Soon after the initial discovery of the caves, the lunar explorers found most of the caves were filled with water. It later turned out most of the vast network of lunar caves were underwater. This made underground travel across the moon by submarine not only possible but necessary.

4. THE ADVENT OF IMMORTALITY began in 1731 when members of a lunar construction crew were investigating the damage of an underground settlement after a massive quake. They accidentally discovered a vast network of caves that stretched all around the Moon. They were also astonished to find that the caves had a breathable atmosphere. But they wondered where the oxygen was coming from.

5. SOON AFTER THE INITIAL DISCOVERY the lunar explorers found the caves were filled with water. It turned out most of the lunar cave network was underwater. This made underground travel across the moon by submarine not only possible but necessary.

6. IT WASN'T LONG before the lunar explorers made an even more incredible discovery of giant mushrooms growing in some of the more remote parts of the cave network. They were what made the breathable atmosphere possible.

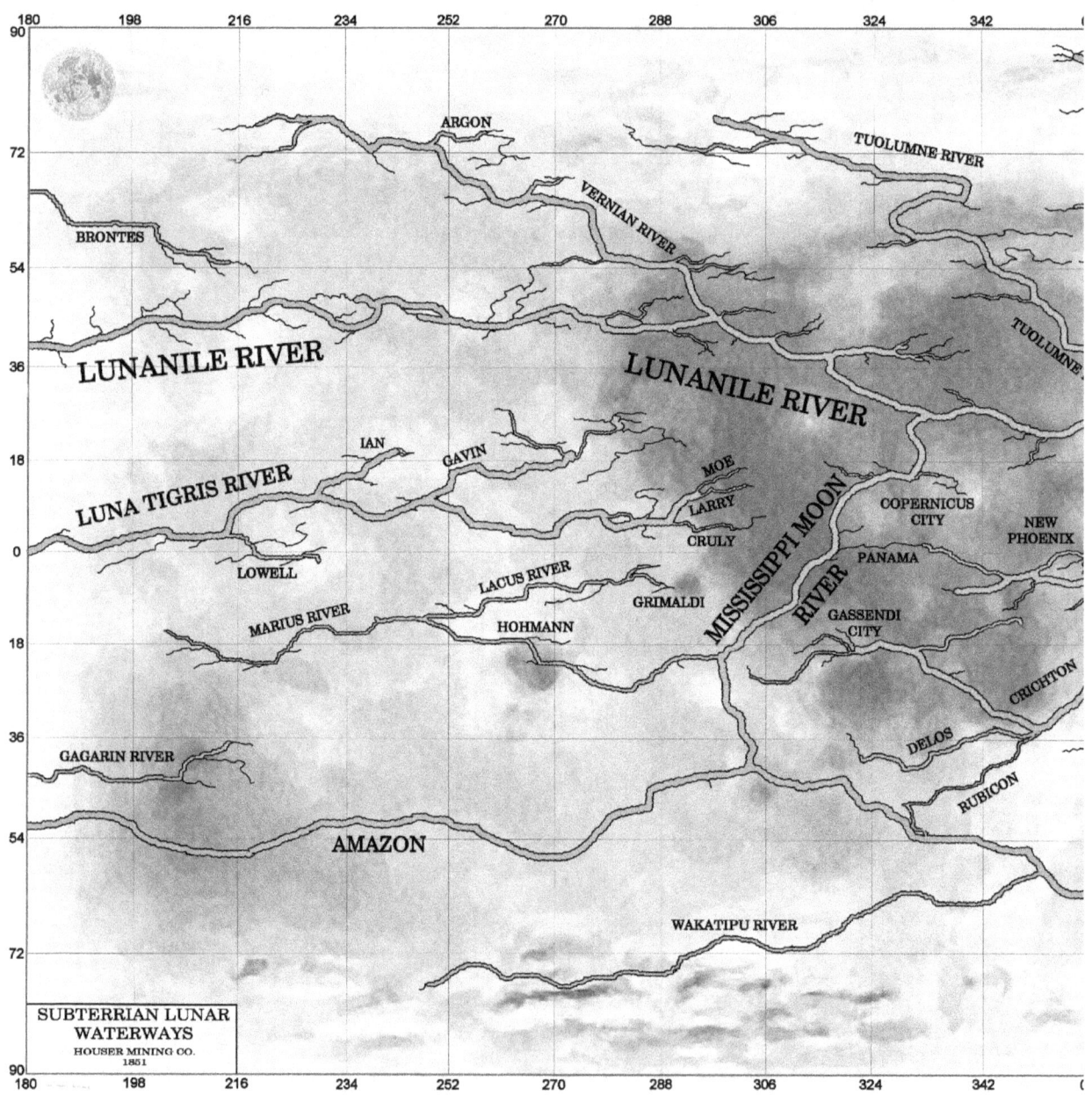

7. OFF WORLD MINING MOGUL Samuel Houser was with the party that first discovered the lunar cave network. By 1751 most of the lunar cave network had been explored and mapped.

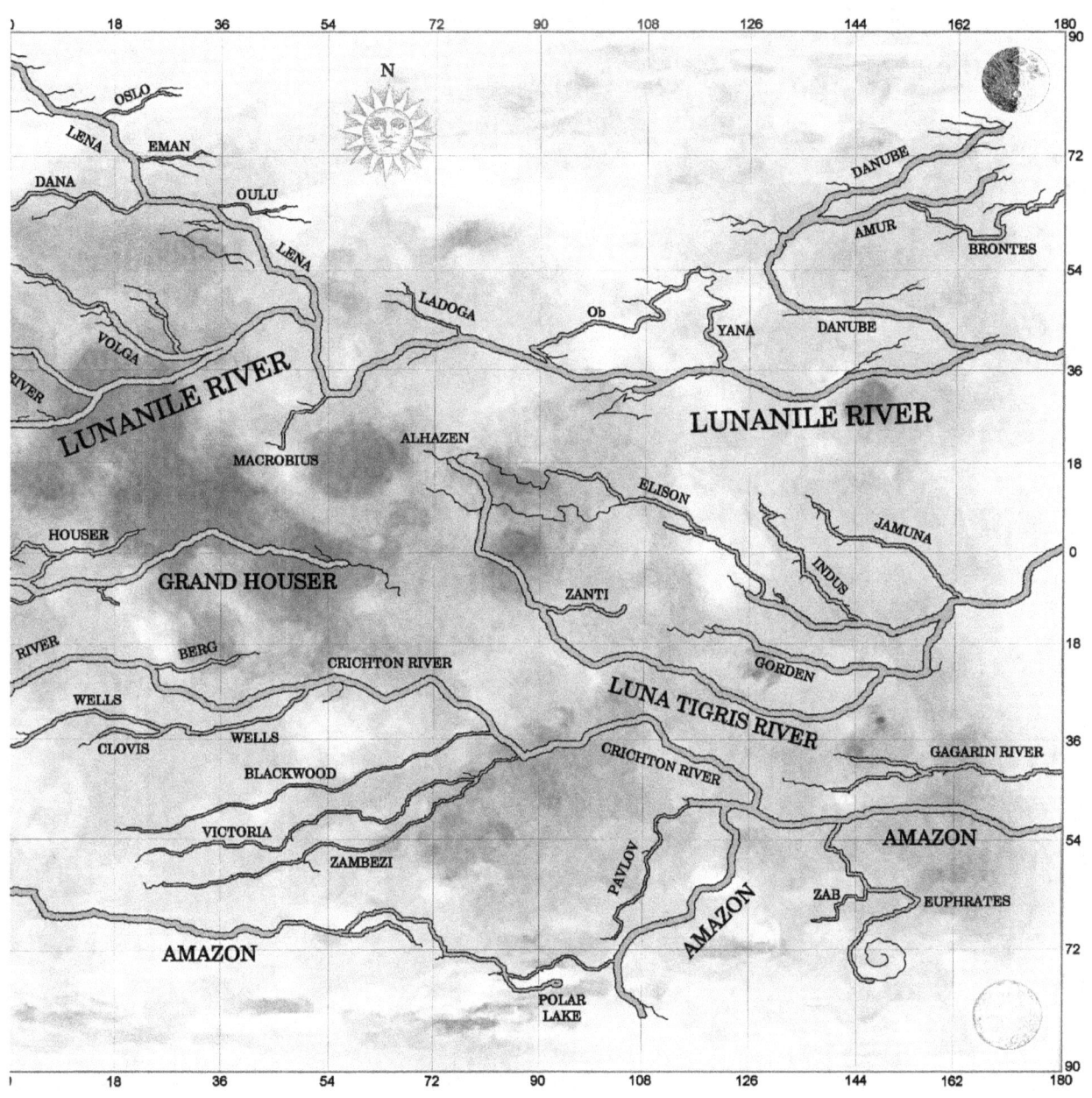

8. ANOTHER INCREDIBLE DISCOVERY came in 1750 when a secluded lunar cave was discovered with mushrooms that were unlike any other. When the first explorers awoke after a night's sleep, they were shocked to see the mushrooms all around grew a likeness of a human face. When Powers Terra learned of the discovery, he became very interested in conducting his own research.

9. **IN 1753, POWERS TERRA** began experimenting with giant mushrooms recovered in caves, deep in the moon's interior. They had powerful imitation and reproduction properties.

Six years later in 1759, after conducting experiments on animals. Powers Terra had perfected a process of complete life regeneration on everything except humans. He considered using a test subject, but the idea faded when he came to the realization that he would have to monitor them for years, possibly years beyond his own life span. He decided to make himself the first test subject, but he couldn't decide when. Regeneration was an incredible discovery, but also a very dangerous one. Terra knew it was something many people would kill for, so he made sure the discovery was kept secret. At this point Terra felt there was no reason for further research until human testing. In the interest of maintaining secrecy, he decided to shelve the project for the time being.

By 1823 Terra was 117 years old. His self-applied earlier life extension treatments had worked, but he was feeling his age. He decided the time had come to attempt the first human regeneration process on himself. It worked. He was now in a much younger body that was approximately 24 years old. The procedure was simple. The subject would lie down on a pad that was made from a specially treated skin of a lunar mushroom. Vapers from the mushroom skin would cause the subject to fall into a deep sleep and hours later wake up in a new body. All that remained of the old body was the skeleton which was easily brushed aside. If a person was old or diseased, he or she could be completely regenerated in a new, stronger body with their memories fully intact. However, there was one distinct difference. The regenerated body was no longer completely human. It was now a plant-animal hybrid. Terra was aware of this from his earlier experiments but wasn't sure of the effect it would have on humans. He planned to monitor himself as the years passed. Having successfully completed the regeneration procedure, Powers Terra faked his death, changed his name to Edward Powers Terra (2nd), and named Edward to receive his full inheritance.

Since the discovery of practical immortality, Terra began thinking about the possibility of establishing an immortal's club at some point in the future. The study of history was a strong interest of Terra. There were many gifted individuals in the past. Terra wondered how much more they could have accomplished had they lived longer.

By 1870 Edward Powers Terra had long established a residence on a remote south sea island he called Eden. Only 3 more years were left on his 50-year life span. His current body was now 71 years old (24 at regeneration plus 47). He could feel his joints getting stiff. There was the occasional tiny plant-like sprout on his arm or leg. It was like a small vine trying to grow from an older larger one. Terra felt the plant side of his body was becoming more dominant. After conducting an extensive self-examination, he concluded that was exactly what was happening. If he didn't renew himself, his plant side would take over completely.

10. **1873, JAMES POWERS TERRA** (now in his third body) looked over the skeleton of Edward Powers Terra (the remains of his second body).

After years of serious thought, Terra felt humanity could benefit from gifted individuals if they were allowed to continue their work beyond their own life span. In 1880 Terra founded the Immortals Club. Because of the risk involved, Terra was careful to oversee each procedure because when the subject was regenerating, they had to be completely alone. If anything, or anyone was with them at the time of regeneration, a hybrid could form. For example: If an animal was in the chamber, the regenerated result would be a person/animal hybrid. Aside from the regeneration process, Terra seldom saw any of the club members and they had no knowledge of each other. Terra was the only one who knew who all the club members were. As a rule, after joining, the club members generally kept a low profile, keeping out of the public eye. Most of them assumed a new identity, usually a younger family member who inherited the entire wealth of their older predecessor.

Another precaution was the location where the regeneration took place. Eden Island was Terra's hidden, private domain. He was the only living person who knew its location. All construction and maintenance on the island had been performed by mechanical servants. Terra selected a remote rocky island outcrop in the North Atlantic. It was very small and had sparce temple ruins from an earlier civilization. By 1879 a small stone building had been erected where the temple once stood. The bridge leading to the coast tower had been restored and loading dock added.

For security, Terra had the island manned by a small group of mechanical workers. When a ship was sighted approaching the island, their job was to release a few lunar cannibal gnats from a concealed green house. Once free they would fly out to the ship. Moments after releasing the cannibal gnats, large mosquito swarms would be released from a second green house. They would follow the gnats out to sea. Minutes later the ship or ships would be swarming with mosquitos. They would turn away and leave soon after. As the ships turned an odor would be released from the cannibal gnats' green house and they would fly back. Terra's ship was the only one allowed to approach and dock, provided he sent the right coded signal. Terra called his island Gilgamesh Island.

It would be the only place members of the immortal's club would know of. The first individual Terra considered for immortality was the brilliant physicist, Margret Dana. She was born in 1798, making her 82 years old by 1880. She was said to be the founder of a new science called interdimensional physics. By this time, she had become so famous she proved very difficult to see. Terra was granted an audience only because if his work in the life sciences. After a long private meeting Dana agreed and became the second living person to visit Gilgamesh Island. After regenerating she became Nancy Margret Dana or N.M. Dana.

11. GILGAMESH ISLAND was the place where Terra established the Immortals Club.

GILGAMESH ISLAND

MAU TONU TEMPLE

SOUTH COVE

EAST HARBOR

N

TERRALANDS
NO. 7
James Powers Terra 1875

0   100
Scale in Feet

12. GILGAMESH ISLAND was the seventh property acquired by Terra. He created an atlas of all his properties. Unlike most maps, Terra's gave no indication of the property's exact location.

13. MARGRET DANA was first chosen by James Powers Terra because she founded the new science of interdimensional physics. **Upper:** In 1820 at the age of 22, Margret Dana had a recorded IQ of 242. That same year her interest in the field of interdimensional physics began. **LOWER:** On October 6th, 1827, Dana's lab assistant, Anna Petrov (wearing an environment suit) successfully stepped through a doorway singularity from California to England and became the first recorded human to do so.

As Ronald Powers Terra (12th) continued to reflect on the past as he looked out over the ocean. He remembered going into past reflection every time before regeneration. It just occurred to him that it was a habit he had developed over the centuries. He looked out at the bright blue star of Venus in the clear early morning sky. Of all his creations, Venus was his greatest achievement and his greatest failure. His involvement with the project began during his 3rd life segment almost 430 years earlier back in 1894. Back then his name was James Powers Terra. At the time, Terra had already become the greatest genetic engineer the world had ever known. He just finished deployment of his latest creation the "Oxroom" plant that was now growing all over Mars.

Terra had no interest in Venus at first. He felt any attempt to terraform Venus would prove far too difficult if not impossible. They once said no one would ever live there. With a surface temperature of 863°F [461°C], a crushing surface pressure of 92 atmospheres, and sulfuric acid rain, Venus was said to be the one world in our solar system most like hell. It was even referred to as the white planet of death.

Yet strangely enough it was the only place off-world where conditions were most Earthlike at an altitude high up in the atmosphere where the pressure and temperature were somewhat like the Earth.

14. TERRA" S OXROOOM PLANT was an engineered plant that would make the Martian atmosphere warmer and breathable, paving the way to the successful terraforming of Mars.

15. **THE FIRST MANNED** expedition to Venus took place in 1783.

16. **THE FIRST VENUS EXPEDITION** didn't land on the planet's surface. Instead, the landing craft deployed gas bags and floated high in the atmosphere for nearly a whole year. During their mission as they traveled the winds all across the planet, they gathered electronic images of the surface and released floating algae platforms. Even though Terra had only a passive interest, he had engineered an algae that was resistant to sulfuric acid. In fact, the entire mission platform was coated with a sulfuric acid resistant material, including the balloon skins.

17. THE BASIC GONDOLA of the first Venus mission was based on the same design as the first manned Mars module from 20 years earlier. When the mission was completed, the crew rode the "Drop Rocket" up to the return ship that had been circling in space overhead.

18. **IN THE YEARS THAT FOLLOWED** the first expedition to Venus, floating settlements were established all across the planet. Because they had no direct contact with the surface, they were like space settlements in many ways. The main difference was that the Venus settlements had gravity, air pressure and temperature like Earth and like space settlements, no two were alike.

19. LIFE ON VENUS was not without fatalities. Once in a great while the engines on a shuttle would fail and without power, the shuttle would glide down into a fireless inferno, burning up long before reaching the surface. When asked about it, and older prominent stately resident casually said, "God never intended us to live here".

For centuries there were individuals who felt it would be possible to change other worlds in a way that would allow people to live out in the open just as on Earth. Unknown to Terra, one of them was N.M. Dana. In some circles she was often referred to simply as Merlin. Dana got that name because her work gave others the impression, she had magical powers. Beyond her involvement in the immortal's club, Dana was also a member of a small exclusive group of extraordinary people, each of which excelled in their own field far beyond known science. Of all of them, Dana might have been the most mysterious. Her work in understanding nature was so profound it was said "God gave her the keys to the Universe". N.M. Dana was never seen in public, and people only speculated about her appearance. When dealing with the public she always had a representative, Richard Chambers.

For Dana one of the biggest problems that had to be solved in order for people to live off-world was to find a way to block the harmful rays of the sun on a planetary scale. Her primary interest at the time was Mars. By 1889, after years of research, she invented a new controllable configuration of energy that could influence only the material desired while leaving everything around it completely undisturbed. She christened it "SEE" (Select Effect Energy). After an intensive study Dana came up with a plan for a practical application of her new discovery. She believed it would make other worlds in our solar system safe from the Sun's harmful rays. Her plan was to convert the two existing mass drivers into high energy cannons reconfigured to fire SEE energy. They would orbit a planet opposite to each other. At the exact moment they would both fire an energy pulse wave directed at the edge of the planet's iron core. In time the core would begin to spin creating a magnetic shield that would protect the planet from the Sun's rays. This would allow life to grow.

After the creation of SEE energy, Dana began to have second thoughts. She believed at some point in the future SEE energy could be reconfigured on a smaller scale to kill people by passing thru armor and disrupting anything behind it.

20. **AS THE YEARS PASSED** Nancy Dana was perhaps the most mysterious of all the members in the Immortals Club from Terra's point of view. As a result of her continued work in interdimensional physics, she had firsthand knowledge of other worlds that would be unknown for centuries.

21. SELECT EFFECT ENERGY is fired through several different materials at Dana's laboratory. One aspect of SEE energy was that it could be re-configured to effect different materials and density depending on the desired application. Extensive experiments proved the possibility of being able to increase the rotation of a planetary core without disturbing the mantel and crust.

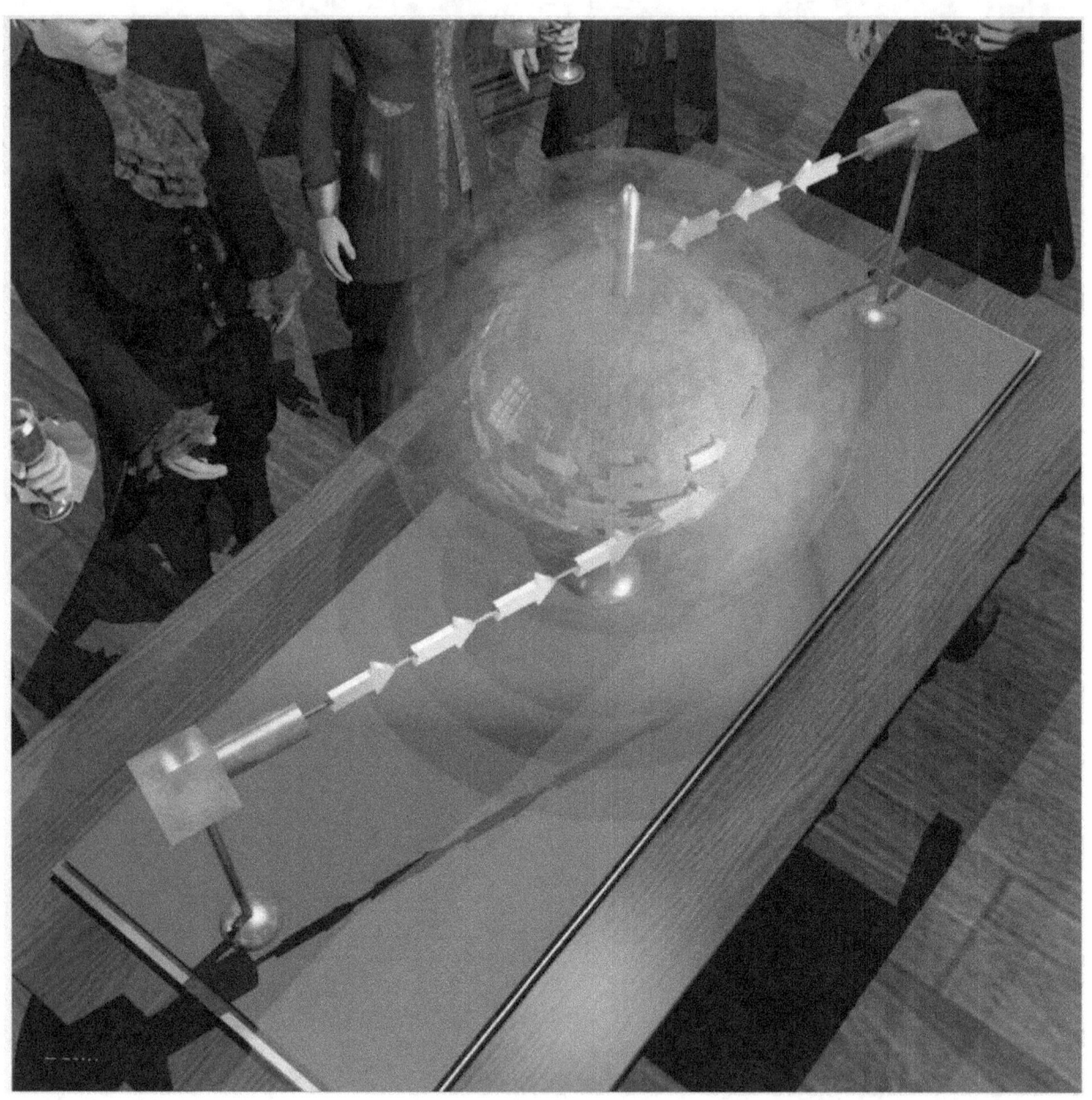

22. IN AN EFFORT for Richard Chambers to explain and persuade the powers that be, Dana had a model constructed that illustrated how SEE energy would be applied to the core of a planet. The increased rotation would create a magnetic shield and in the case of Venus, could create an approximate 24-hour day. Note: The size of the model's core was over exaggerated to increase effect visibility.

23. **PLANETARY MINING MOGUL ALEXANDER ELIAS DELOS** had mining operations throughout the solar system. He had a long interest in the possibility of terraforming Venus. His interest wasn't in habitation as much as making the planet less hostile for automated mining. After learning of the SEE energy demonstration, he sought an audience with Chambers. Delos had a liaison with Terra and was also a member of the Immortals Club.

On August 9th, 1897, Chambers met with Alexander Delos. To Chambers surprise, Delos was a younger man who looked to be somewhere in his mid-30's. Chambers wondered how someone his age could accomplish so much. Delos told Chambers he studied the application of SEE energy on Venus's proposal and was very excited about the possibilities. Chambers was even more surprised to learn that Delos had already secured two mass drivers for modification. When Chambers reported back to Dana, it was more than she could ever hope for, and yet after hearing the details of the meeting, there was something about Delos that made her feel uneasy. It was as though Delos would stop a nothing to see the project go through at any price.

It wasn't long until word of the Venus Proposal spread throughout the entire solar system. There was strong resistance from most of the floating cities on Venus and from people everywhere who had family members living in those cities. Terrance Waverly, a longtime resident of the floating Venusian city New Sumarros lead the collation to stop the project. Delos did a personal planet wide tour of every Venusian floating city (except the ones he owned) to promote the project and ensure its safety. As he and his party traveled across the floating cities of Venus, Terrance Waverly followed close behind, giving opposition speeches and presentations. By August 1898 Delos had persuaded all the floating cities of Venus to green light the project.

Two years later in 1899 the first practical application of SEE was put to the test, but not on Mars. Instead, Delos insisted on Venus because if anything went wrong, the planet was considered uninhabitable to begin with. He had little doubt there wouldn't be any effect on the floating cities. He decided to be aboard one of the mass drivers when the time came. By mid-September 1899, the two converted mass drivers reached Venus and circled the planet opposite each other awaiting the orders to fire.

24. TERRANCE WAVERLY'S life came to a tragic end after the grand explosion rocked New Sumarros on July 7th, 1898. His body evaporated long before reaching the lower atmosphere. Shortly after the event, all the local opposition leaders withdrew their objection to the Venus Project.

On October 12th, 1899, the order came, and both mass drivers fired what looked like a small bright star directed at the edge of the planet's iron core. Just as Dana predicted the star like ball of SEE energy passed harmlessly through the cloud tops, through the lower atmosphere, and into the surface without any disruption effect. It was almost like a 3-dimensional phantom image as it passed by the floating settlements in the Venusian atmosphere. Cities near the event were given blinders and told to look away as the ball of energy passed by. Moments later both balls of SEE energy became active as they struck the planet's core from opposite sides and directions at the exact same time. All was quiet for a moment, then there were massive earthquakes all over the planet. From space the cloud tops showed little effect. In the months that followed, the quakes subsided, and the floating cities reported stronger winds, but nothing they couldn't handle. Close surface measurements indicated the effect was exactly as Dana had calculated. On occasion there were still powerful aftershocks all over the planet. The rotation of Venus was changing. In 5 years, the planet will have an approximate 24-hour day. But that wasn't all. The increased movement of the core was generating a magnetic field that would become strong enough to block the sun's harmful rays. The planets axial rotation and orbit were stable. It worked!

The world was ecstatic. For the first time people everywhere began to wonder about the real possibility of a second Earth in the solar system. In recent years there have been many fantastic accomplishments but nothing on a planetary scale of this magnitude. For the next several weeks, the news of Venus was in every newspaper around the world. Despite what had just happened, Venus was still a hot and hellish place and after a few months the world forgot about Venus.

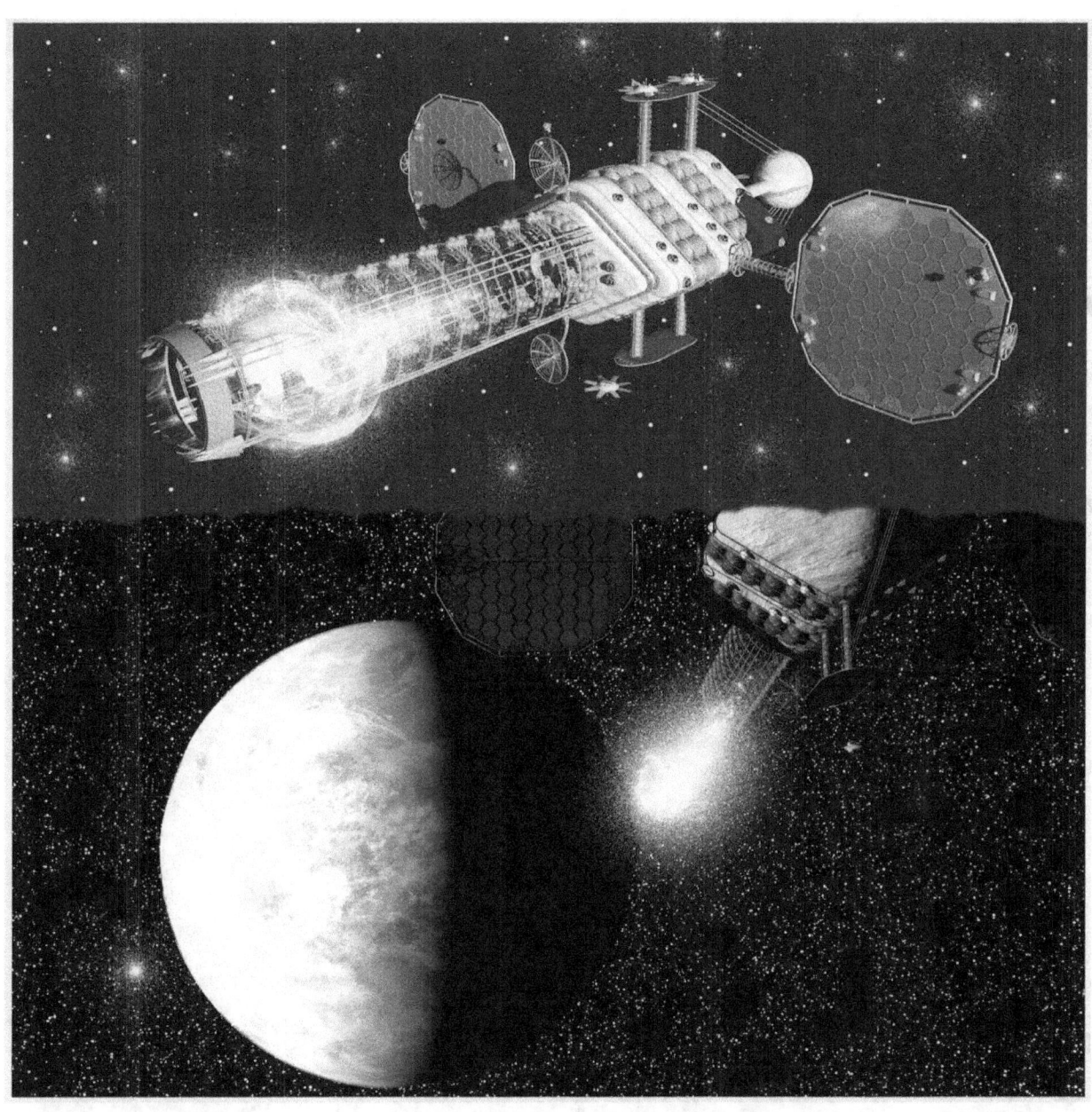

25. **WHEN THE TRUE POWER** of select effect energy was released on Venus, all other worlds watched with excitement and fear. Some described it as a controlled cataclysmic event.

Like the rest of the world, Terra gave little thought to Venus as he went about his work in the greenhouse. His latest project was to grow houses and buildings that people could live and work in. Terra was intrigued with the idea of growing a home or building that could renew itself.

26. JAMES POWERS TERRA had been a master of life science for many years. Intrigued with the idea of living buildings and houses, he conducted experiments in his Greenhouse.

Terra read that his friend Alexander Cristos Delos was behind what was happening on Venus. Terra remembered inviting Delos into the Immortals Club back in 1880 because of his work in off-world development. He was 58 at the time he joined. He was Alexander Elias Delos at the time. After going through re-generation, he became Alexander Cristos Delos. Terra believed if humanity was to survive it had to expand beyond the Earth. Delos was one of the major players in that effort. Terra knew sooner or later he would hear from him. Now that planetary conditions on Venus could become favorable, it was only a matter of time until Delos would seek Terra's services to create another terraforming planet miracle, just as he did on Mars.

It was October 12th, 1900, exactly one year after the Venus event (as it was later called). The day on Venus was now 157 Earth days. Terra received word Delos wanted a meeting. In early November the meeting took place at Terra's residence on Eden Island in the South Pacific. Terra was surprised by Delos's appearance. He was not the same person he remembered. Delos explained he had been in a terrible accident years earlier and had to undergo reconstruction. As Terra looked closer, he could see the resemblance to the man he remembered. He scolded Delos for not seeing him in the first place, claiming no one was better than him for the reconstruction task.

After the issue was put aside, Terra expected and received a hard sell from Delos to except a commission to develop a life form that would help terraform Venus. Most of the public didn't know all the details of how much the planet had changed since the event. On occasion there were still massive quakes all over the planet. The weather was changing, although not by much. The once consistent global weather was not quite so locked in a predictable pattern. The massive quakes all over Venus broke up its hardened surface exposing under soil. Some believed this was somehow affecting the temperature and weather, even if it was only by a negligible amount. Terra was fascinated by the details of Venus but didn't think it was possible to create anything that would grow there.

Terra had given considerable thought to it already. The one thing he couldn't get past was the intense heat and crushing pressure. To his knowledge, no known life or even the molecules of life's building blocks could survive in such a harsh environment. Once exposed, they would simply break down instantly. He thanked Delos for his visit but declined his offer.

27. **IN EARLY NOVEMBER 1900**, James Powers Terra met with Alexander Cristos Delos on Eden Island. Terra was surprised by Delos's appearance. He was not the same person he remembered. Delos explained he had been in a terrible accident years earlier and had to undergo reconstruction.

It was 1901, two years after the mass drivers had fired on the planet's core, Venus was spinning faster now. The Venusian day was now 97 Earth days. The weather was still changing but posed no threat to the floating settlements. There was still no explanation for the slightly cooler surface temperatures all across the planet. Sense the beginning, Delos was curious about what kind of minerals one might find on Venus. Massive quakes had cracked open the hard baked surface and exposed deep Venusian soil. Delos thought it would be a good opportunity to have mechanical workers explore some of the deeper sites and recover ore samples. By now the quakes were becoming less frequent and less intense. By June of 1902 Delos had selected several sites to collect ore samples. The first was a deep fissure that opened at Citlalpul Vallis. Months earlier a quake created a grand chasm that was miles deep. Delos felt it was the best place to get a look into the interior of Venus.

In addition to his other interests, Delos operated several off-world penal colonies. It was a big business and controlling dangerous criminals was much easier in environments harmful to life. He had one facility on Venus that he named after himself. First established in 1895, it was a floating penal colony that housed 5000 inmates. As one might expect it was an ominous place like a dark floating castle. It was also the only place where he could carry out his operations. Until now Delos only had limited involvement with any kind of surface activity. In late 1902 he began several ore sample excavation missions. They were expensive unmanned operations. Even with the slightly cooler temperatures, Venus still had a very hot suppressive atmosphere. The average life span of a mechanical worker was only 23 hours. Despite providing small shelters (Furnace Modules) that were kept cool so repairs could be made, the mortality rate of mechanical workers was still very high, and they managed to fry at an alarming rate. As expected, the progress of collecting soil samples was very slow.

Another promising mining site was in the Maxwell Mountains. Delos had the Delos prison facility tethered directly over the site in 1903. The high altitude of the Maxwell Mountains made it possible to have a much shorter tether than in most other places. The tether had a length of 43 miles [69.2 kilometers]. A month after the mining site was founded, the surface settlement became known as Elysium Donte.

28. **THE CITLAPUL VALLIS** fissure was the first site Delos chose to land an expedition of mechanical miners.

29. **THE OUTDOOR FURNACE** at Elysium Donte where mechanical workers fry at an alarming rate under the crushing atmospheric pressure and intense heat.

A typical Furnace Module

30. **THE MAIN BUILDING BLOCK** of most surface settlements on Venus was the Furnace Module. It was designed to be a safe haven within a furnace environment. They were typically dropped into a site by parachute and are used primarily as a maintenance garage for mechanical workers. They extended the life of a worker approximately four- and one-half times, from 23 hours to 103.5 hours. The module's interior is cooled to 130°F [54.4°C] and the air pressure is reduced to five atmospheres. The Module is powered by the outside heat and can be interconnected. The module's outer ceramic skin protects against the hash corrosive atmosphere of Venus. The outer pressure door is used as a draw bridge after landing.

31. **A FURNACE DOME** section is lowered down to Elysium Donte. Delos wasn't satisfied with the short life of mechanical workers on the surface of Venus. In an effort to improve conditions he believed if the underground mines could be cooled, atmospheric pressure reduced and filled with a non-corrosive mixture of gases, it would greatly extend the life of workers and equipment. To achieve the desired result a 12 section Furnace Dome was built to cover the mine entrance at Elysium Donte.

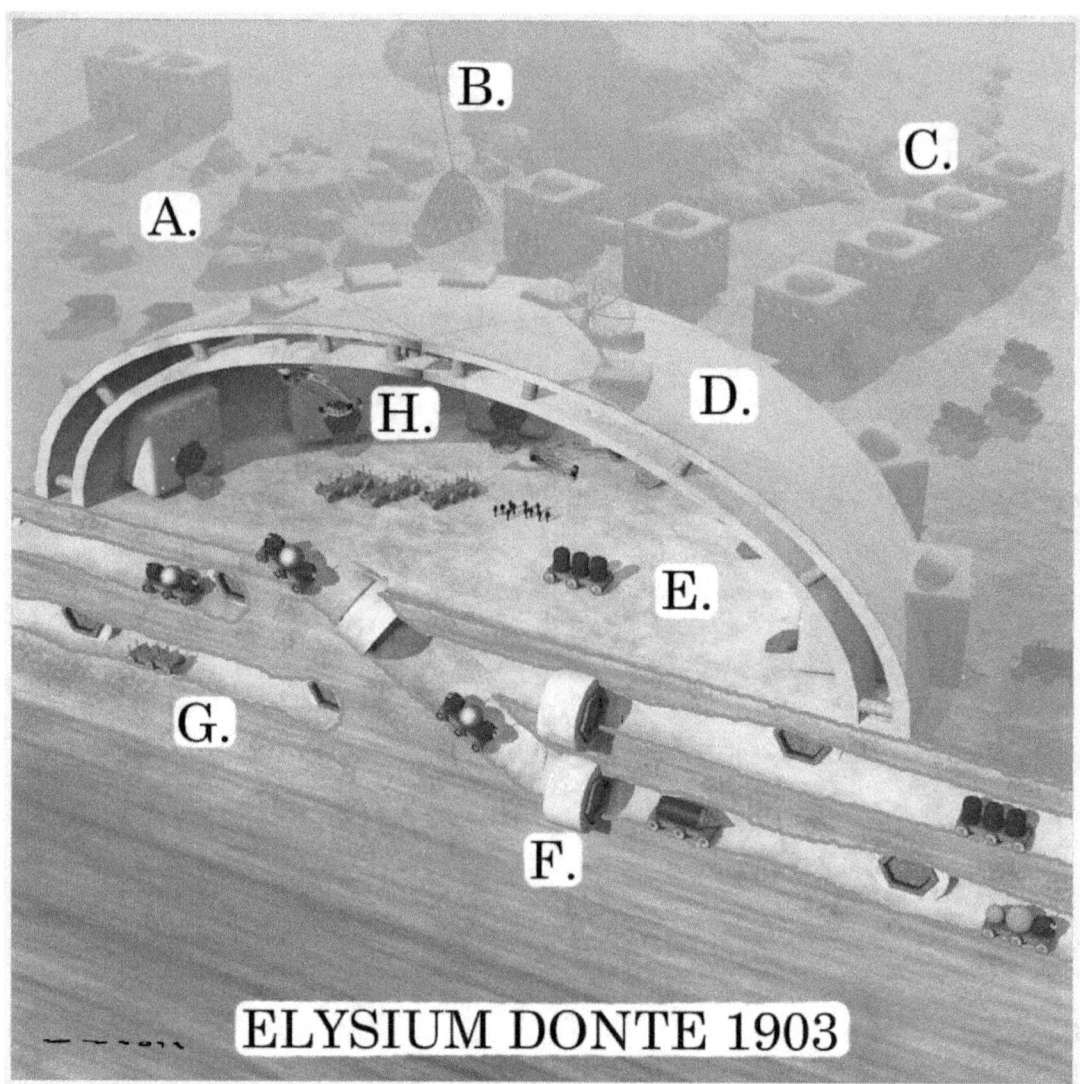

ELYSIUM DONTE 1903

32. ELYSIUM DONTE 1903 was highlighted by the newly completed Furnace Dome that dominated the settlement. **A.** The outside temperature and pressure at Elysium Donte was 716°F [380°C] and 45 bars. **B.** A nano tube tether keeps the floating settlement Delos in place several miles overhead. **C.** Furnace Modules. **D.** The Furnace Dome. **E.** Inside the Furnace Dome and the mine tunnels below the temperature and pressure is kept at 80°F [26.7C] and 1 bar. It also has a breathable atmosphere of an oxygen/nitrogen mix. This was something Delos wanted to allow for occasional human visitors. **F.** Air Lock Pressure Doors are located throughout the tunnels to ensure safety in the event of an atmospheric breach. **G.** Free from the crushing pressure and temperatures outside, mining operations can operate as they would on Earth. **H.** After a Furnace Dome section is assembled in place, most of the landing supports are converted into overhead cranes.

On July 30th, 1903, Delos was reviewing notes from the latest ore samples. The results revealed more than he had hoped for: hydrogen! For Delos the irony of his dream was the most abundant element in the universe was thought to be almost nonexistent on Venus and yet, if Venus was to be terraformed, hydrogen would be essential. Since the very beginning he believed it existed somewhere on the planet. After the discovery, he was almost ecstatic. After years of patient research, he found the one element that would be the key to his dream. It turned out early in Venus's history, when the planet surface was starting to heat up, vast amounts of hydrogen ore became trapped under the hard baked surface of the planet's crust, although the theory of exactly how it happened would be the subject of debate for years to come.

Early November 1903, exactly 3 years to the day after their first meeting, Delos met with Terra for a second time. Terra was delighted to see Delos but still only had passive interest in Venus. When Delos revealed the Venusian soil samples Terra was impressed by the endurance of the mechanical workers who retrieved deep samples under the harshest conditions. He thought the hundreds, perhaps thousands of workers must have fried in the heat. Terra agreed to examine the samples but made no promises that he would have any involvement. The biggest selling point for Delos was the abundance of hydrogen in the Venusian soil. Once combined with oxygen, it would make vast amounts of water possible, paving the way for life and eventually a true second Earth nearby.

As Terra examined each of the samples using an electron microscope, he discovered a curious pattern in many of them. There were areas embedded in the stone that appeared to be under greater compression than the surrounding stone. These areas existed as clusters much in the same way cancerous cells exist in healthy tissue. A closer look revealed the condensed areas were composed of hexagon tube structures that were clustered in groups like tall city buildings. In his journal Terra also described how the building clusters (as he referred to them) were interconnected by a vast network of thin hair like tubes similar to the way cities on Earth are connected by roads. Further tests revealed the hair tube strands were highly conductive. Terra couldn't free himself from the feeling he had been examining a fossil or dead tissue.

33. 1903, **JAMES TERRA** examines the latest soil samples from Venus.

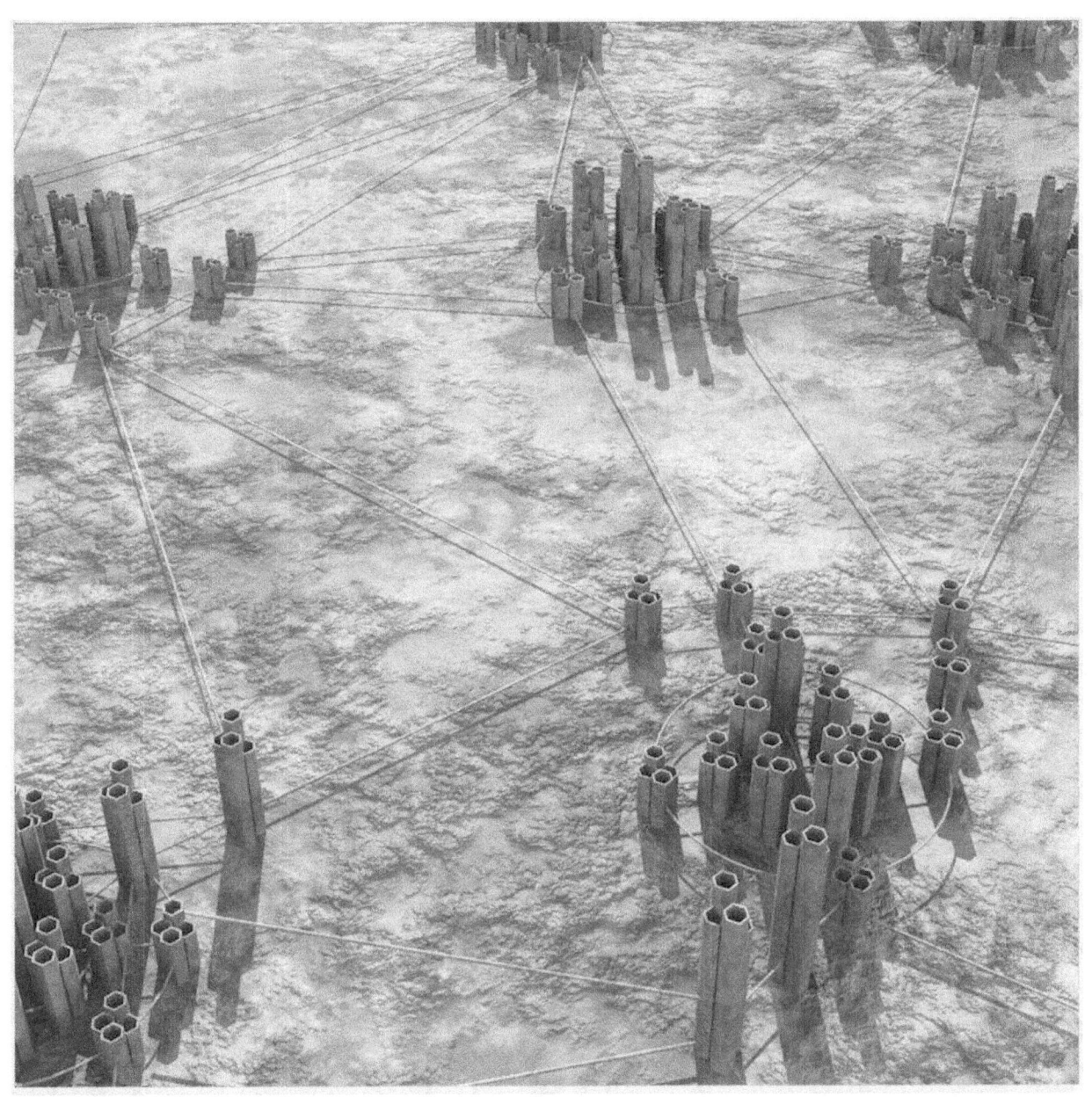

34. **UNDER EXTREME MAGNIFICATION** unnatural patterns appeared in the soil samples from Venus, shown here in false shading.

Despite all he had accomplished, Terra started to feel his work was limited. Something about the Venusian soil samples changed his thinking. He started to believe it might be possible to engineer a life form to terraform Venus after all. But to do it he would have to go beyond his scope of life definition.

Terra knew no life (no carbon-based life) could endure the hellish environment of Venus for any length of time unless it had the properties of stone. This meant it would have to be a carbon/silicon hybrid. Only then it could survive. This would give it the ability to grow and resist the environment at the same time. And over the course of time, change that environment to become more earthlike. Terra knew if he was successful, it would be perhaps his greatest achievement. It would prove once and for all his fundamental belief that all things were possible through life engineering. Five days after their meeting, Terra contacted Delos to accept his proposition, but made no promises. Terra made it very clear that he would only investigate the possibility of creating a carbon/silicon life form. Even though he had no assurances from Terra, Delos was very pleased that the next phase of his plan for the Venus project was falling in place.

In the months that followed Terra became a recluse and no one, not even Delos, could see him. In a way, Delos might have expected it. He remembered an earlier time when he heard of Terra going into seclusion before announcing the development of a life form that could terraform the Martian atmosphere. Alone in seclusion, Terra slowly began to focus on his new hybrid life form. As a means of recreation and to clear his mind Terra often spent time just off Eden's shore beneath the sea. The sea reminded him of the thick Venusian atmosphere.

As his submersible passed through a kelp forest, Terra got his inspiration of what would be the final form of his new creation. A week later Terra had worked out the general life form's size requirements in his mind. He felt, for his new creation to work, it had to grow very tall. This would allow it to affect different levels of the atmosphere in different ways at the same time. To be effective it would have to reach an altitude of approximately 67 miles [108 kilometers]. To firmly anchor such a tall plant in place, the base would grow to become a small hill measuring approximately 400 to 600 feet [122 to 183 meters] in diameter with a height of up to 300 feet [91 meters]. Its roots would borrow deep beneath the surface to reach and absorb the Hydrogen in the soil and securely anchor the stalk. The crushing surface heat of Venus would provide the planet with massive amounts of energy required to grow and sustain its interaction with the atmosphere. The stalk itself would be composed mostly of interconnecting lighter-then-air gas cells that would support the bulk of its weight as it grew. The top of the stalk would be a grand balloon cluster that would help insure and support the stalk's height in the thin upper atmosphere of Venus. At approximately 40 miles up, above the clouds of sulfuric acid, where the air and pressure are suitable, large hallow globular island-like structures would form on the stalk to support massive amounts of algae to begin the process of converting carbon dioxide into oxygen. Down in the clouds below, the stalk would have charged lightning rods to break down sulfuric acid. Terra called his new creation Furnace Kelp.

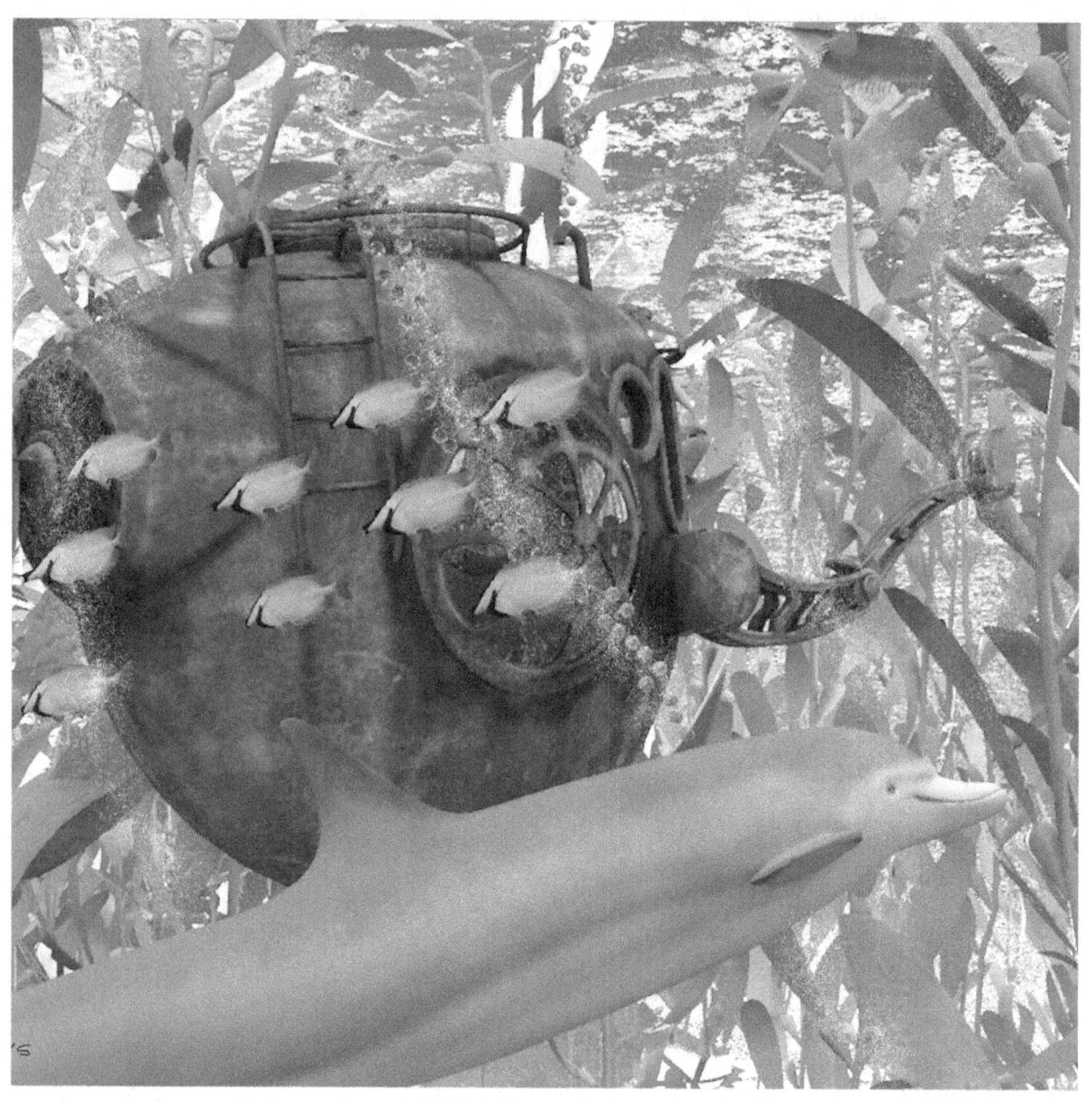

35. SUBMERGED IN A KELP FOREST of the coast of Eden Island, Terra got the inspiration for the new life form that would terraform Venus.

As Terra continued to research the possibility of creating Furnace Kelp, he started to think of what its life cycle should be. Assuming such a creation could terraform the atmosphere of Venus to become more Earth like, what then? Would this life form create an environment where it could no longer survive? After thinking about where a similar condition would exist in nature, Terra soon realized it was nothing new. An example was a person that has a terminal disease eventually dies. After killing its host, the disease also dies. So would be the case of Furnace Kelp. Terra felt after the kelp had died off, it could be used for a building material for the future cities that would rise on an earthlike Venus.

After reaching a conclusion of what the life cycle of Furnace Kelp should be, Terra created renderings. They illustrated the birth, life, and eventual death of his new life form. As he looked at them, Terra realized he was looking at a living stone structure that was changing its form over time. He also realized for Furnace Kelp to survive it needed energy, vast amounts of energy. Of all the things said about Venus, the one thing it had in abundance was energy.

So far Terra had only worked out the general parameters of what Furnace Kelp needed to be. The very heart of the problem was working out the life form's matrix on a molecular level. Only then he would find out if it was possible. It was January 1904. Terra, still living in his 3rd body was now 198 years old, yet despite his age, the problem before him made him feel like a kid with a new toy. Alone on Eden Island, Terra went into seclusion as he immersed himself in solving the matrix problem. Over the next two years Terra was able to create a carbon/silicon hybrid life form that would grow in the harsh environment of Venus. In the lab, everything had to be done at a greatly reduced scale. Another factor was that the new life form would grow only in soil brought back from Venus. Terra concluded to prove out the Furnace Kelp concept, a scale plant would have to be grown in a much larger simulated environment. After further study he later concluded the prospect of constructing a scale model of the Venusian atmosphere was not possible. There was no way to grow a single Furnace Kelp through all the various atmospheric levels without separating it into tanks.

36. **BY 1906 TERRA WAS ABLE TO GROW** small test samples of Furnace Kelp in a lab enclosure that recreated the surface environment of Venus. The kelp would only grow in Venusian soil.

37. **THE LIFE CYCLE OF FURNACE KELP** in the first 100 years of growth. Terra envisioned the Furnace Kelp life cycle in steps based on a timeline of years after the initial planting. **1.** In the first 30 years after planting the base of Furnace Kelp would grow to become a small hill measuring approximately 400 to 600 feet [122 to 183 meters] in diameter with a height of up to 300 feet [91 meters]. Its roots would borrow deep beneath the surface to reach and absorb the hydrogen in the soil and securely anchor the stalk. **2.** Approximately 40 to 60 years after planting the first lighter than air sacks would appear. **3.** By 80 years the plant's balloon air sacks should have grown much larger, possibly reaching a height of 1000 feet [304.8m] **4.** By one century after planting the balloon cluster separated from the base, revealing the kelp stalk.

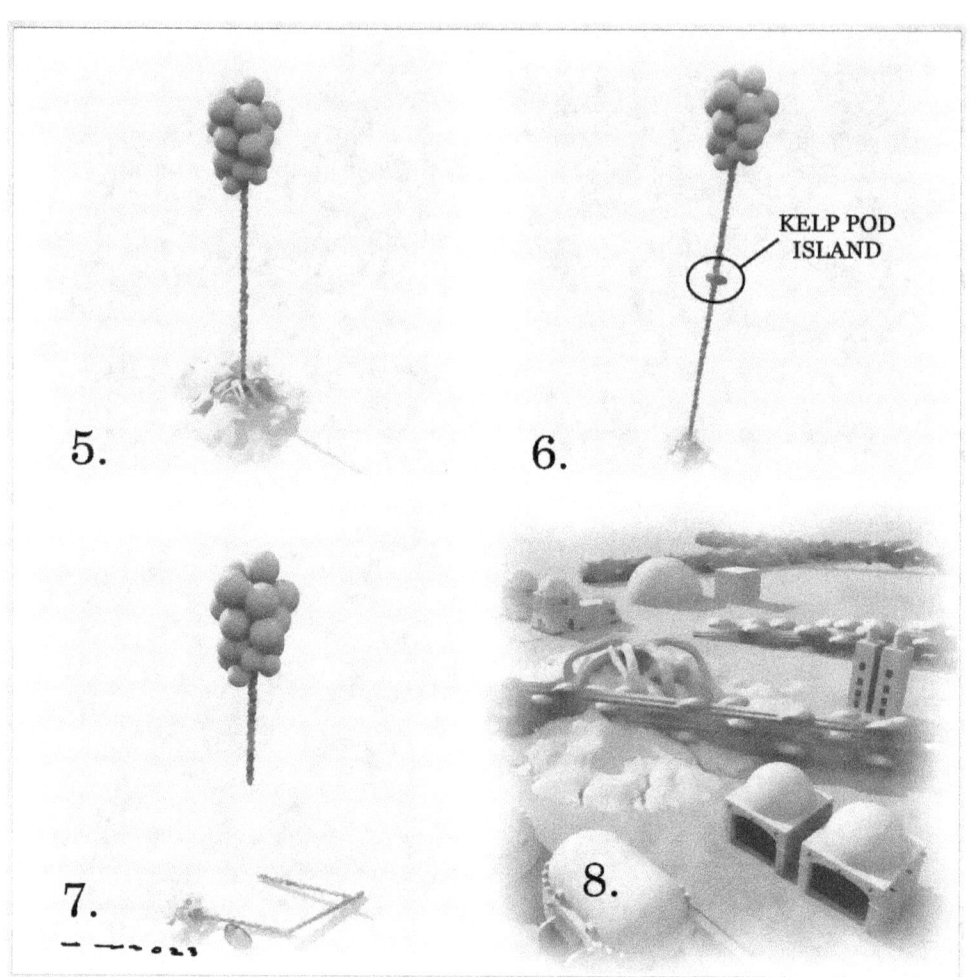

38. **THE LIFE CYCLE OF FURNACE KELP** after the first 100 years. **5.** In the 2nd century after planting the height of furnace kelp would be measured in miles as the stalk continues to grow. Most furnace kelp should be reaching the mid atmosphere. By now the process of breaking down sulfuric acid has begun. **6.** The kelp pod island should form approximately 350 years after planting. The pod island growth is at an approximate altitude where the temperature and air pressure are close to that of Earth. **7.** Somewhere between 500 to 1000 years the atmosphere of Venus has become earthlike. It is now breathable. The sulfuric acid is gone. The thin atmosphere of Venus can no longer support Furnace Kelp. As a result, the kelp begins to break up and die. The balloon cluster will likely be the last remaining part of the kelp as broken off sections continue to float in the upper atmosphere for a brief time before falling to the surface. **8.** The dead stonelike material of Furnace Kelp provides an excellent building material for future habitation.

In July of 1906 Terra came out of seclusion to meet with Delos. Even though Terra felt he made only limited progress in the past two years, Delos was excited with the results. Terra felt the project had come to a standstill unless a way to grow a scale model of furnace kelp could be found. Terra also explained that even if a way to reproduce a scale model of the Venusian atmosphere could be found, the cost of such a project was far beyond his means or the means of anyone he knew of. Delos assured Terra if the project was possible, the cost would not be a problem. At that point Delos revealed that he was a member of the Venus Consortium.

Upon hearing this, Terra was somewhat alarmed. Who was the Venus Consortium? And why had he never heard of it? Terra was able to conceal his general reaction. As Delos started to explain what the group was about, Terra quickly concluded the Venus Consortium was merely an extension of a small powerful group of world oligarchs that controlled most of the affairs on Earth. Terra referred to them as "The Shadows" because they used the bulk of the wealth to conceal their identity. Terra had known about them for some time and considered them very dangerous. Knowing Delos had some involvement with them made Terra very uneasy. He knew he would have to change the way he regenerated in the event he was killed before being able to surrender his memories to the next body.

Delos assured Terra the cost of developing furnace kelp would not be a problem and closed their meeting by praising Terra for his work so far. After Delos left Eden Island, Terra was still faced with the same problem. How can a miniature version of Venus' atmosphere be recreated on Earth? Terra had to create a miniature Venus atmosphere with all its different pressures and temperatures, all in the same long vertical space. And had it not been for Dana, his longtime friend, it wouldn't have been possible, and Terra would have canceled the project. Terra would never forget how the solution to his unusual problem came about.

In a correspondence with Dana, he shared his problem of trying to recreate a 1/300 scale, miniature version of Venus' atmosphere contained within a 1000-foot tower. Terra described growing his kelp through a series of interconnecting tanks, one above the other, each with its own atmospheric conditions. It would be impossible to stop them from leaking into each other, but it was the best scenario he could think of. Not long after, he received a message from her saying that the answer could be found at the Gateway statue and asked him to meet her there.

The Gateway Statue was an underwater location off Eden's south coast. Answering her invitation, piloting his one-man submersible, Terra set it down near the underwater stone gateway on a sandy clearing just beyond the kelp forest. Looking out at the Gateway he noticed a small device positioned at its base. It consisted of a metallic cone with a sphere on top.

Suddenly a bubble of air formed around the sphere. Unlike normal bubbles, it didn't rise to the surface. Instead, it stayed centered around the sphere and rippled slightly as it reacted to the water around it. Then it started to expand. As it did so the pocket of air grew. Soon it became so large it engulfed Terra's submersible. He began to feel trapped! Without water he couldn't move. Then the bubble stopped growing. Both his submersible and the Gateway were now inside a bubble of air. He was tempted to open the hatch but fearful because he was still clearly under the sea.

On the far side of the Gateway something was moving in the kelp forest just beyond the bubble wall underwater. It was a diver making their way through the kelp. The diver stepped through the bubble wall slowly and walked up to the submarine. After looking directly into Terra's porthole, the diver removed her helmet. It was Dana! She smiled and motioned him to open his hatch. Terra was both amazed and shocked to meet her this way.

Minutes later he was out, standing on the seabed floor, speaking to her directly. There he learned Dana had perfected, at least in part, another practical use for SEE energy. It was capable of creating a displacement almost anywhere. It emanated from the sphere and this time it affected only the sea water around them. Oxygen was allowed to remain so they could breathe. Its range was exactly that of the bubble displacement. Terra later described it as a kind of force field.

Dana explained after receiving his correspondence, the problem was recreating a miniature version of Venus' atmosphere, all in a single vertical space. She said the solution was to employ the use of SEE energy. It could create individual displaced areas layered on top of each other, and each could have its own temperature, pressure, and gas composition. This would allow Terra to recreate a miniaturized version of the Venusian atmosphere in a tower. But it was not without warning. Dana warned the artificial displacement field wasn't as secure as she would like, but even with that factored in, it was still far better and less expensive to maintain. Dana would allow Terra the use of SEE for his application but wanted it kept secret. Terra agreed. Dana referred to her force field as a "Tankless Atmosphere".

39. **THE TANKLESS ATMOSPHERE** is shown to Terra for the first time at an undersea location off the coast of Eden Island.

Dana's tankless atmosphere was the final technical key needed to complete the development of Furnace Kelp. With the last part of the equation in place, Terra was able to create detailed plans of the Venus atmospheric project he called "The Tower of Venus". The last thing needed was funding. Delos was ecstatic when he received news of the Venus Tower. Terra later received word that the Venus Consortium requested a presentation on Furnace Kelp before granting funding. Terra agreed to give the presentation, but the thought of going before these people made him very uneasy. He felt he was going before the Devil himself. Terra was flown by Delos to a hidden location in the Swiss Alps.

40. THE VENUS CONSORTIUM agreed to give an audience with Terra at a location in the Swiss Alps. It was a place known only to a few as The Black Castle.

FURNACE KELP IN THE VENUS ATMOSPHERE

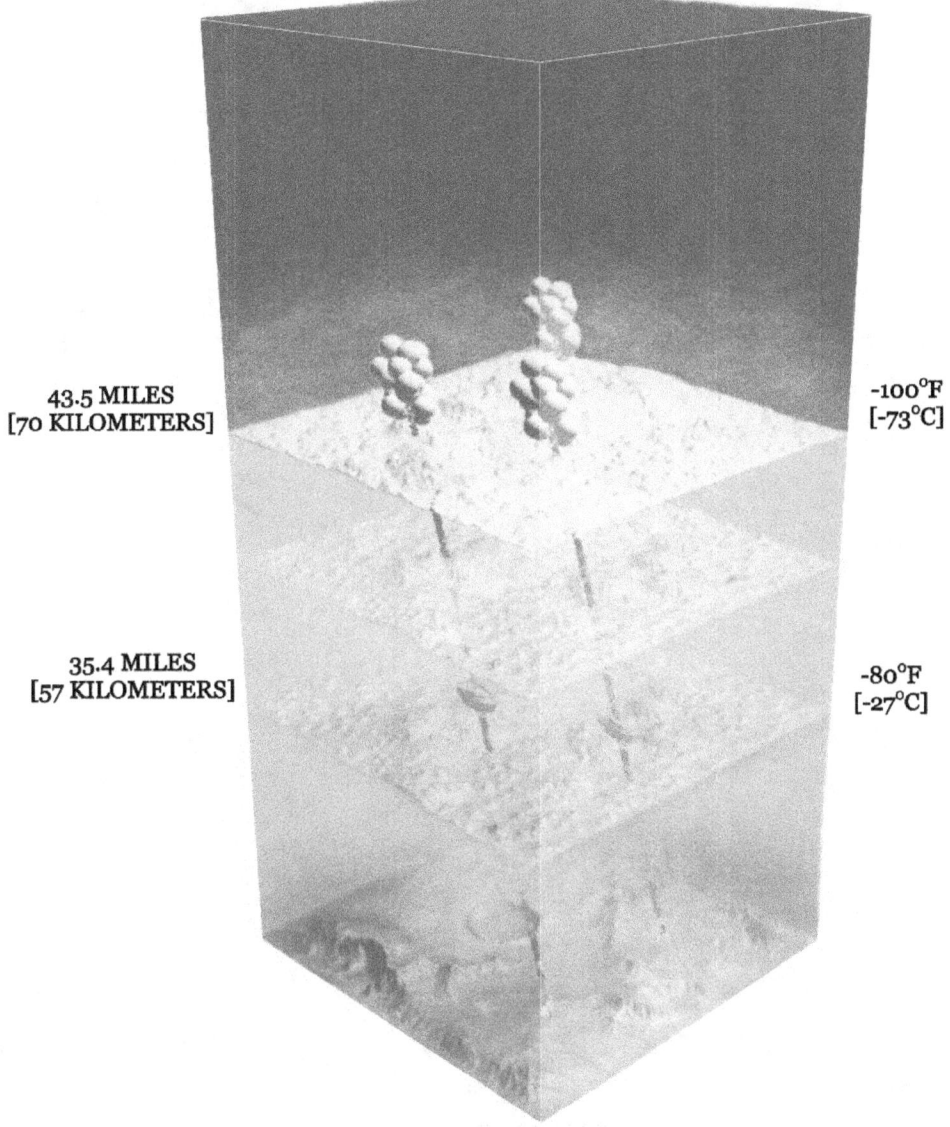

43.5 MILES
[70 KILOMETERS]

-100°F
[-73°C]

35.4 MILES
[57 KILOMETERS]

-80°F
[-27°C]

SCALE: NONE

41. TERRA'S PRESENTATION began by illustrating what mature Furnace Kelp in the atmosphere of Venus would look like.

42. MATURE FURNACE KELP terraforming and dominating various levels in the atmosphere of Venus. The middle image shows the kelp pod islands located in the upper atmosphere where air pressure and temperature are close to that of Earth.

FURNACE KELP POD

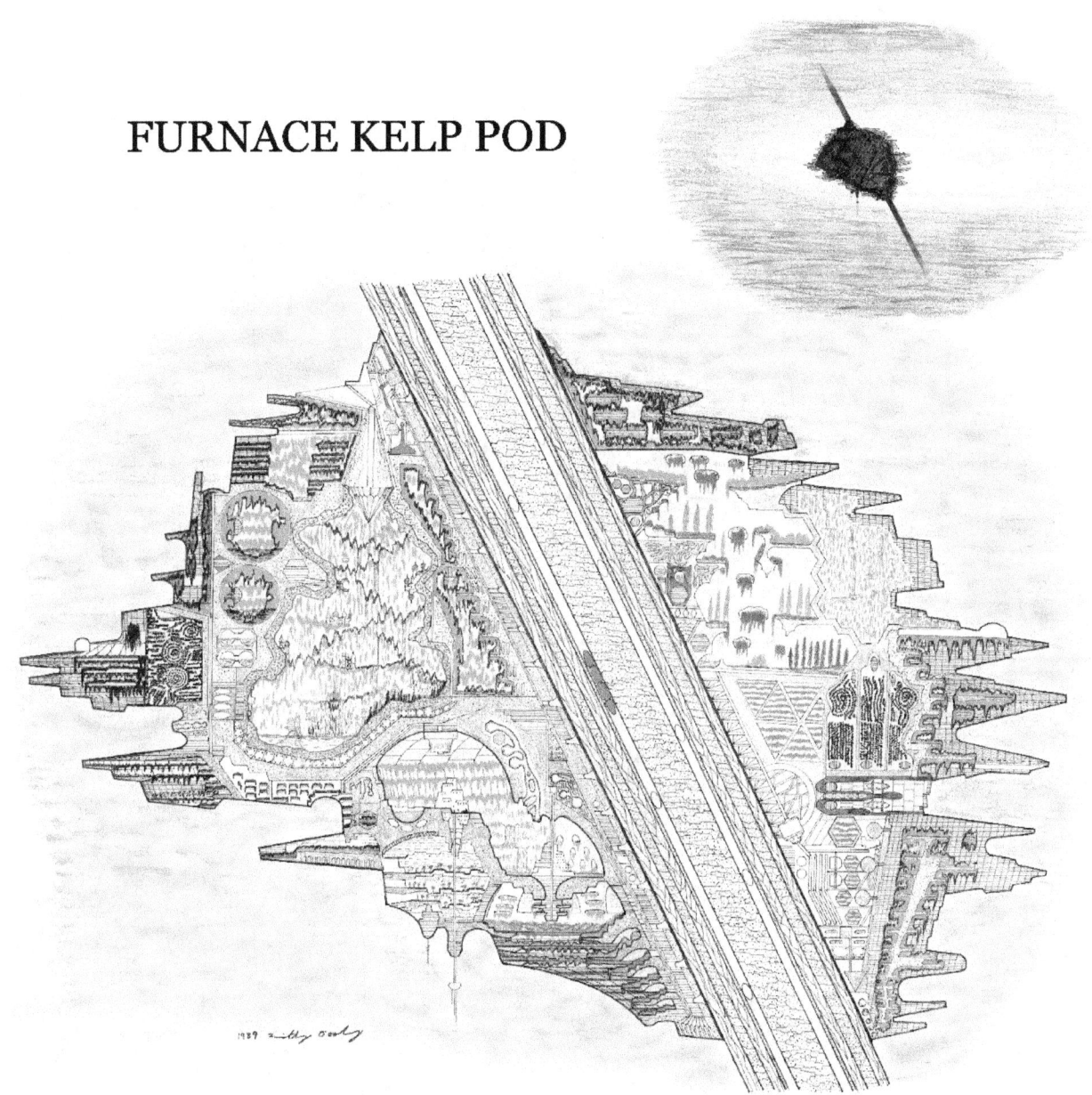

43. **AN EARLY RENDERING** of a Furnace Kelp Pod. Terra suggested the Kelp Pods have vast amounts of plants that would help convert the carbon dioxide air of Venus into oxygen. Terra also suggested the kelp pods could be used as temporary settlements to house the kelp farmers.

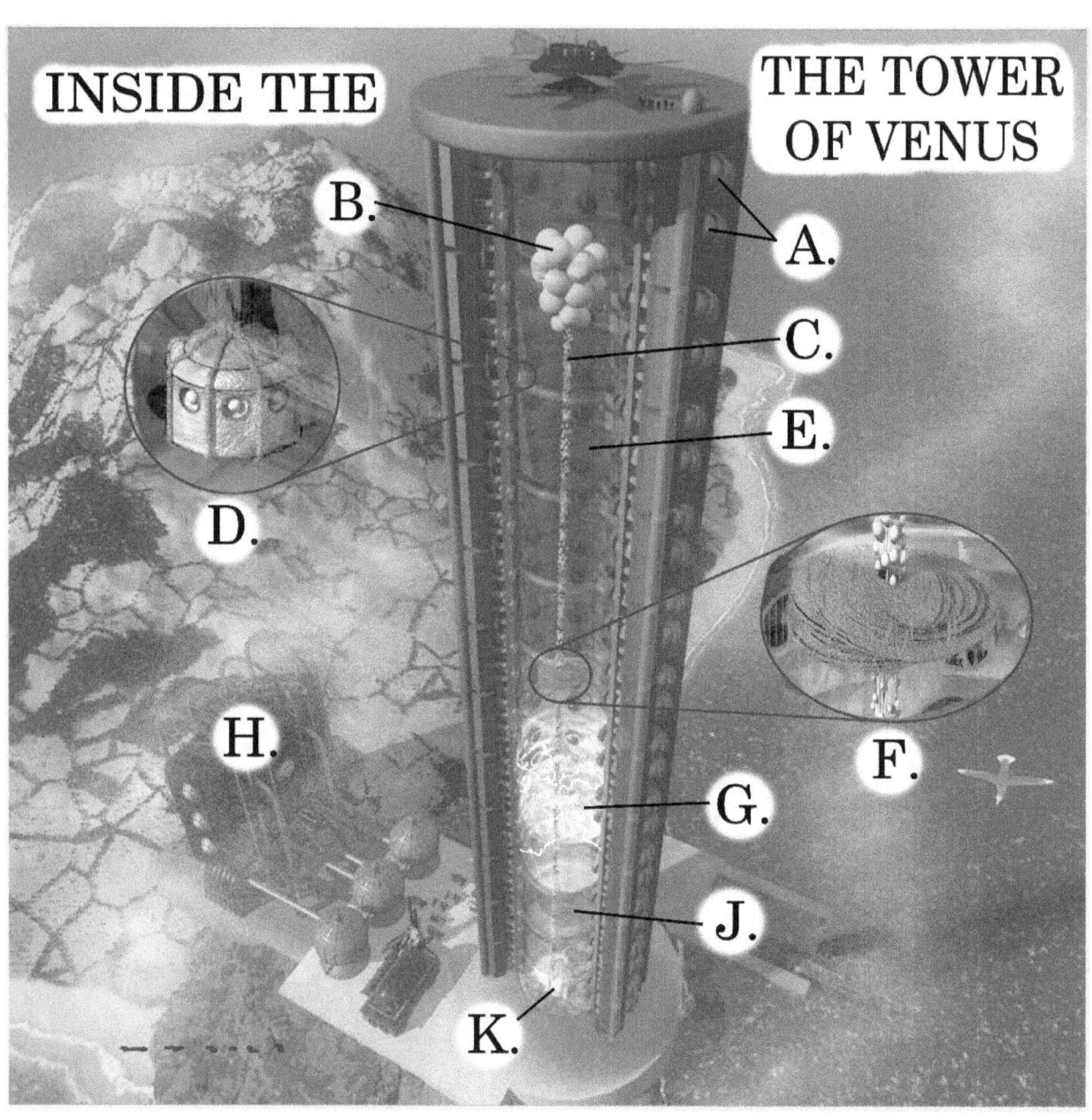

INSIDE THE

THE TOWER
OF VENUS

A.
B.
C.
D.
E.
F.
G.
H.
J.
K.

44. **INSIDE THE TOWER OF VENUS** gave a general overview of Terra's proposal. It was a cutaway of the thousand-foot tower that showed a single furnace kelp growing in a 1/300 scale, miniature of Venus. **A.** Atmospheric ducting vents are in each of the tower's twelve modules. Each module has eight ducting vents. They simulate air currents at different atmospheric levels. The tower has a total of 96 ducting vents. **B.** The lighter than air balloons at the top of furnace kelp keep the grand stalk upright and they also deposit water vaper in the upper atmosphere. **C.** The furnace kelp's grand stalk. The scale version in the tower reaches approximately 950 feet [289 meters]. When grown to full scale on Venus, the stalk length should reach an average length of 54 miles [86.8 kilometers] **D.** The tower's core diving bell allows up to four people to observe furnace kelp up close as it grows. It provides a pressurized, temperature-controlled environment that protects its occupants from the cold vacuum of space at the tower's top, all the way to 800°F [426°C], 90 atmospheres of pressure at the tower's bottom. **E.** The internal core of the tower simulates the various atmospheric levels of Venus by having twelve separately controlled environments stacked one on top of the other. **F.** At an altitude where air pressure and temperature are similar to Earth, the furnace kelp pod forms. It is like a floating island that is covered in plant growth that helps convert the cardon dioxide of Venus into oxygen. It is also a place where a settlement for the kelp farmers could be located. **G.** In the lower-mid atmosphere, highly conductive spikes growing of the stalk break down sulfuric acid by means of lightning. **H.** All mixtures of gases that match those found on Venus are produced by an atmospheric processing plant. It also changes the mixtures as the tower's core is influenced by furnace kelp to become more earthlike. **J.** An example of atmospheric levels in the tower is the third section up from the base. It has a pressure of approximately 34 atmospheres and a temperature of 662°F [350°C]. It reflects a scale altitude of 10.4 miles [16.7 kilometers]. **K.** The tower floor is a direct model of the surface of Venus. To accurately reflect the kelp roots ground penetration a hole 250.5 feet [76.4 meters] was dug and filled in with soil from Venus.

TOWER OF VENUS MODULE

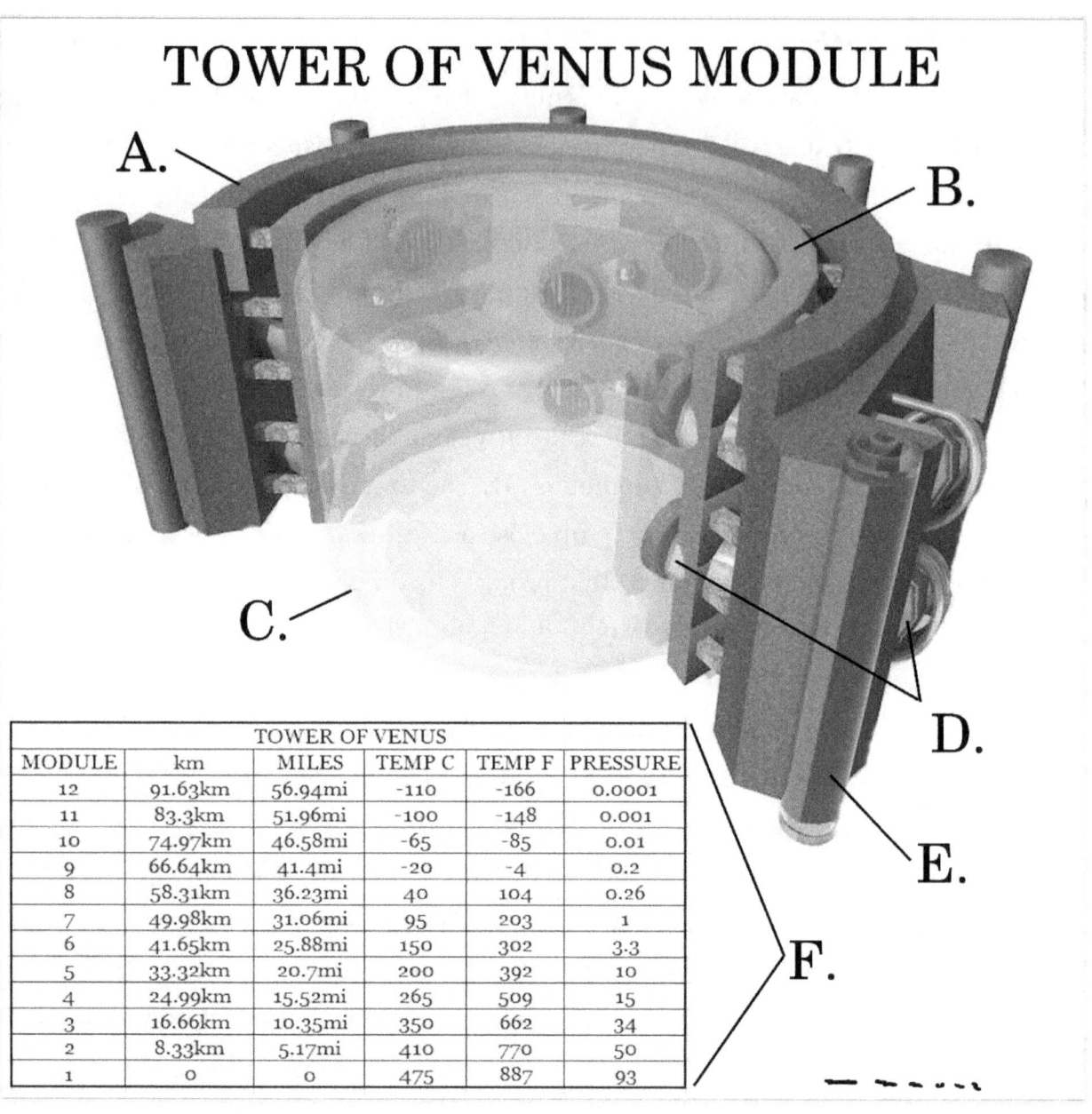

A.

B.

C.

D.

E.

F.

TOWER OF VENUS					
MODULE	km	MILES	TEMP C	TEMP F	PRESSURE
12	91.63km	56.94mi	-110	-166	0.0001
11	83.3km	51.96mi	-100	-148	0.001
10	74.97km	46.58mi	-65	-85	0.01
9	66.64km	41.4mi	-20	-4	0.2
8	58.31km	36.23mi	40	104	0.26
7	49.98km	31.06mi	95	203	1
6	41.65km	25.88mi	150	302	3.3
5	33.32km	20.7mi	200	392	10
4	24.99km	15.52mi	265	509	15
3	16.66km	10.35mi	350	662	34
2	8.33km	5.17mi	410	770	50
1	0	0	475	887	93

45. **THE TOWER OF VENUS** was basically an assembly of 12 modules. Each module had a height of 83.33 feet [25.4 meters] and represented a scale altitude of 25.080 feet (4.75 miles) [7.6 kilometers] in the Venus atmosphere. **A.** Tower's outer core. **B.** Tower's inner core. **C.** Tankless atmospheric section. **D.** Atmospheric ducting (eight per module). **E.** Glass elevator tube. **F.** Module pressure and temperature chart.

Terra was somewhat relieved when his presentation was over. Even though he wanted to move forward with the tower project, he was uncomfortable being in the presence of the Venus Consortium. He wanted to leave the Black Castle as soon as possible. He was there only briefly. The whole time he was there, Terra saw only Delos and a few servants helping him. When Terra gave his presentation, he was allowed only on a small stage under bright lights and couldn't see the people he was addressing who sat in the darkness beyond. Delos was always at stage side and asked all the questions. Terra noticed Delos looking into the darkness and motioning his head as though someone in the darkness was directing their questions through him. Terra was quickly escorted off the stage when the presentation was over. Minutes later he was back aboard the shuttle with Delos and flown away.

As they flew back to Eden Island, Terra's mind was not on the presentation he just gave. He was thinking about taking steps to ensure his own future safety. Terra had been to the Black Castle. He had gone before the shadows. Now they knew who he was by name and his friend Delos was in league with them. Terra wondered just how deeply Delos was involved with the Shadows. Could Delos be trusted? Terra began to feel he had gone before the face of evil itself. He felt he needed to take a shower.

After returning Terra to Eden Island, Delos gave words of encouragement before he departed. Nearly 2 years passed before Terra heard back from Delos. Terra had mixed emotions during that period. He wanted the Furnace Kelp project to go forward but felt a sense of relief if the Venus Consortium had no interest in him or his work. Shortly after he returned to Eden Island, Terra searched the world for another remote site to have a safe house where he could regenerate when the time came.

Terra discovered an island off the coast of Antarctica that would be ideal for a safe house. He dedicated his time to converting the island to meet his needs.

46. AVALON ISLAND off the coast of Antarctica became the secret location where Terra could regenerate. The entire facility was completed in June 1908. **Upper:** from the surrounding sea, Avalon appeared as nothing more than a cluster of ice-covered rocks. **Lower:** The crater interior of Avalon Island was suitable for an artificial greenhouse environment. It took Terra's mechanical army nearly two years to build Avalon Castle, the greenhouse and steam towers. A variant of the tankless atmosphere blocked any detection from space.

47. AVALON ISLAND was the 19th Earth property acquired by Terra. As he was establishing his new home and greenhouse, Terra continued having thoughts of creating a new way to regenerate that would allow him to continue if he was killed.

In early August 1908 Terra heard from Delos with news that the consortium wanted to go ahead with the Venus Tower Project. Having moved most of the critical infrastructure related to his personal work off the island, Terra was less concerned about having temporary construction workers on Eden Island. He made sure their presence was restricted only to work areas and the coastline. Those who ventured into the island's interior were never heard from again.

48. **BY 1909 THE TOWER OF VENUS** begins to rise on Eden Island. Delos didn't visit too often. He made sure the money kept flowing in as needed. When news of the tower came out, many ocean vessels crossing the Pacific altered their course to see the tower from a distance as they passed by.

49. DELOS PRISON was where Alexander Delos spent most of his time while on Venus. Tethered to Elysium Donte, 31 miles [50 kilometers] below, it was the closest safe place to check up on his local mining operations. By 1909 the facility was in its 14th year of operation.

50. ALBERTO SANTOS WAS Delos's right-hand man for all operations on Venus. He ran both Elysium Donte and Delos Prison. Back in 1903 after the Furnace Dome was in place, Santos organized a prison work force for the mines of Elysium Donte. This greatly reduced the cost of machine maintenance. Santos had a following among the prisoners.

51. BY SUMMER OF 1910 the Tower of Venus was now visible from miles away.
Photographs taken from passing ships were in newspapers all over the globe. It was
becoming clear to the world; humanity was deeply engaged in the goal of creating a
second Earth in the solar system. Everyone following the development on Venus
marveled that it had an approximate 24-hour day.

52. DELOS MET WITH SANTOS after visiting Elysium Donte. The mining operations were not going as well as Delos had hoped. The under soil of Venus had unique electrical properties, but it wasn't enough to make the daunting task of mining and transporting it off-world profitable. By 1911 all mining operations at Elysium Donte were shut down.

Delos was excited to receive an invitation from Terra to visit Eden Island. It was now March 1916; eight years sense the project began and three years sense the Tower had been completed.

53. **EDEN ISLAND** in 1916 after the Tower of Venus was completed. The island was Terra's third holding on Earth. Terra quietly referred to his estate holdings as Terralands.

54. **AS DELOS APPROACHED EDEN ISLAND** by sea, the Tower of Venus could be seen from miles away. Delos didn't appreciate the tower's immense size until he stood outside the elevator at the base. The thousand foot [305 meter] tower pierced the low coastal clouds as they passed overhead.

Shortly after his arrival, Delos and Terra boarded a hover falcon and flew to the tower's top. Terra had the pilot slowly circle the tower as they ascended. As Delos looked out it was clear that the Tower of Venus may very well be the most technically advanced building in existence. Terra assured him a perfect miniature 1/300 scale atmosphere of Venus had been successfully recreated in the tower's core. The hover falcon landed on the tower's large flat roof. There was a slight wind as they stepped out and walked over to the roof entrance. It was somewhat strange that Delos had a fear of heights considering where he spent much of his time back on Venus. The tower's absence of windows and network of massive pipes and coils gave Delos the impression that it was a gigantic smokestack.

They entered, stepped down a flight of stairs and passed through the pressure doors of an airlock. Soon they were in a small pod suspended from the ceiling over the tower's core. Terra closed the pod's airtight hatch. As the pod disconnected from the docking collar it swung back and forth slightly from its overhead cables. Delos was a little alarmed at first, but Terra reassured him he was in no danger. Looking at the pod's gauges, Delos could see they were 987 feet [300.8 meters] up. The temperature outside was -166°F [-110°C] and the air pressure was 0.0001 of Earth. Another gage indicated Venus's altitude- 56.9 miles [91.6 kilometers]. Terra adjusted the pods inside air and temperature. As he pulled a small lever the pod slowly descended into the tower core. Looking out through the frosted pod windows Delos could see the top of a tree-like structure that consisted of balloons grouped together. They looked to be made of smooth white stone. As he looked closer, he could see the balloons were holding up a stalk that had the appearance of bamboo woven into a thick single vertical vine. Its skin texture had the appearance of white stone. The vine was covered with many tiny balloon sacks. Terra gave a full explanation of furnace kelp as they descended.

55. **AT A SCALE ALTITUDE OF 65.9 MILES** [91.6 kilometers] Delos and Terra could see the top of furnace kelp as they descended into the tower core. The balloons were secreting water vaper into the atmosphere.

As the pod descended the air pressure and temperature increased. At 833 feet [254 meters] up (46.6 miles [75kilometers] scale altitude), Delos could see large pod clusters of algae growing off the stalk. The temperature was -85°F [-65°C] and the air pressure was only one tenth that of Earth. Terra pointed out the algae growing on furnace kelp was converting carbon dioxide into oxygen. Delos could see flashes of light coming from below as the pod descended into a heavy mist of sulfuric acid. Delos drew back from the window. Terra assured him they were safe, and it wasn't time to replace the pod's windows just yet. As they got lower the pod was rocked with lightning and thunder. Here, the furnace kelp stalk had spikes growing out of it. They were the source of the electrical discharge. Terra pointed out the interaction of sulfuric acid and furnace kelp's metallic elements also produced hydrogen, an element badly needed in the Venus atmosphere if it is to change. Terra had discovered a way to break the acid down to produce more oxygen.

As they descended further, the lightning diminished and once again it was quiet. It also got much hotter, and the air pressure increased. Delos had the sensation that they were underwater. They were now 416 feet [126.7 meters] up (20.7 miles [33.3kilometers] scale altitude). The indicated temperature was 392°F [200°C] and the pressure was almost 10 atmospheres. Terra explained they had entered the upper layer of the troposphere. Outside the texture of the furnace kelp looked rockier. Later the pod came to a stop 5 feet [1.5 meters] off the chamber floor. The outside temperature was 887°F [410°C] and the pressure was 93 atmospheres. The furnace kelp base was like a cluster of stacked river rock surrounded by stone like vines forming into the stalk above. Terra cautioned that they couldn't stay long. Delos was awestruck by Terra's ingenuity.

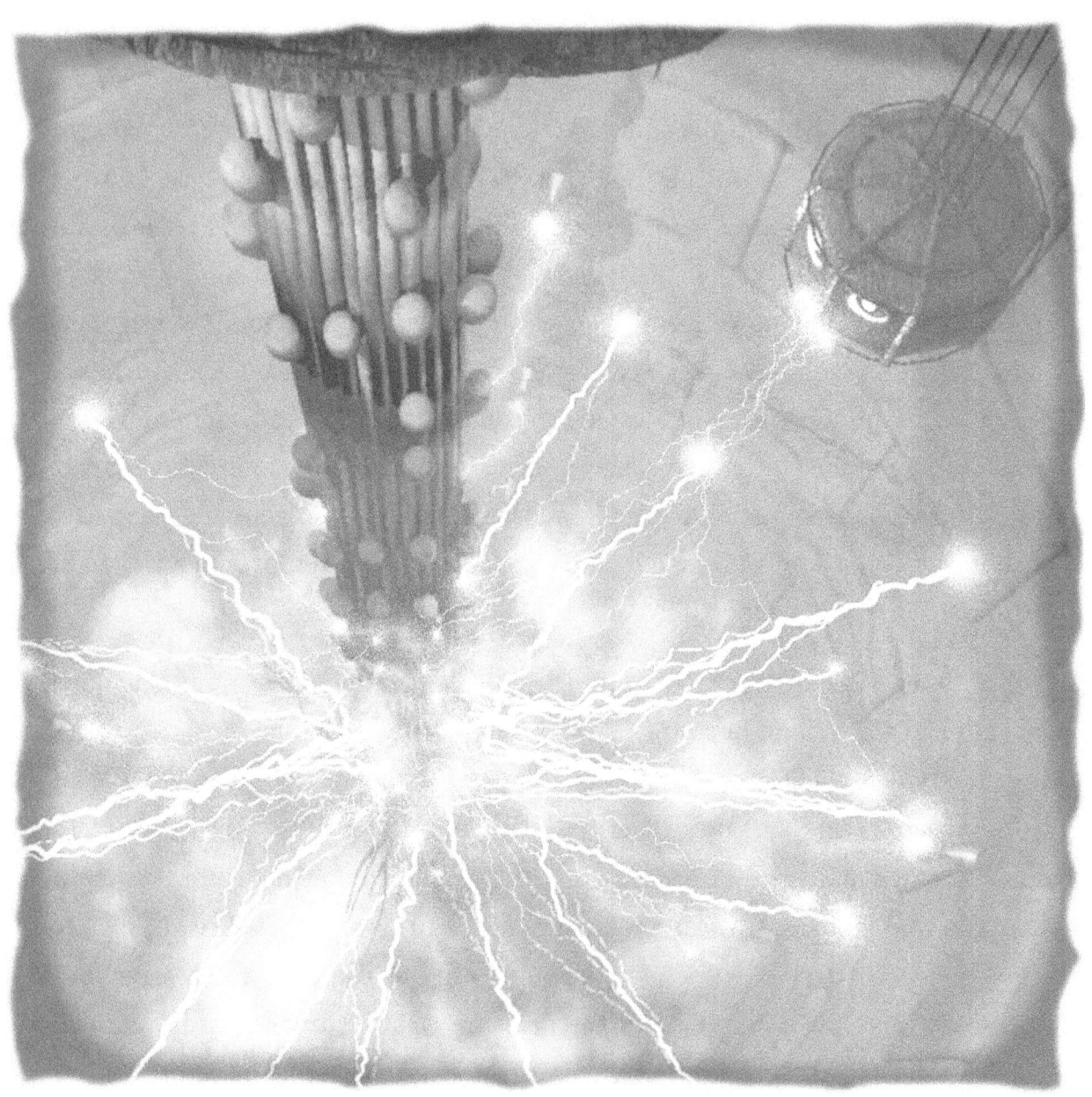

56. AS THEY DESCENDED through the miniature Venusian atmosphere, Delos was amazed at how Terra was able to create it.

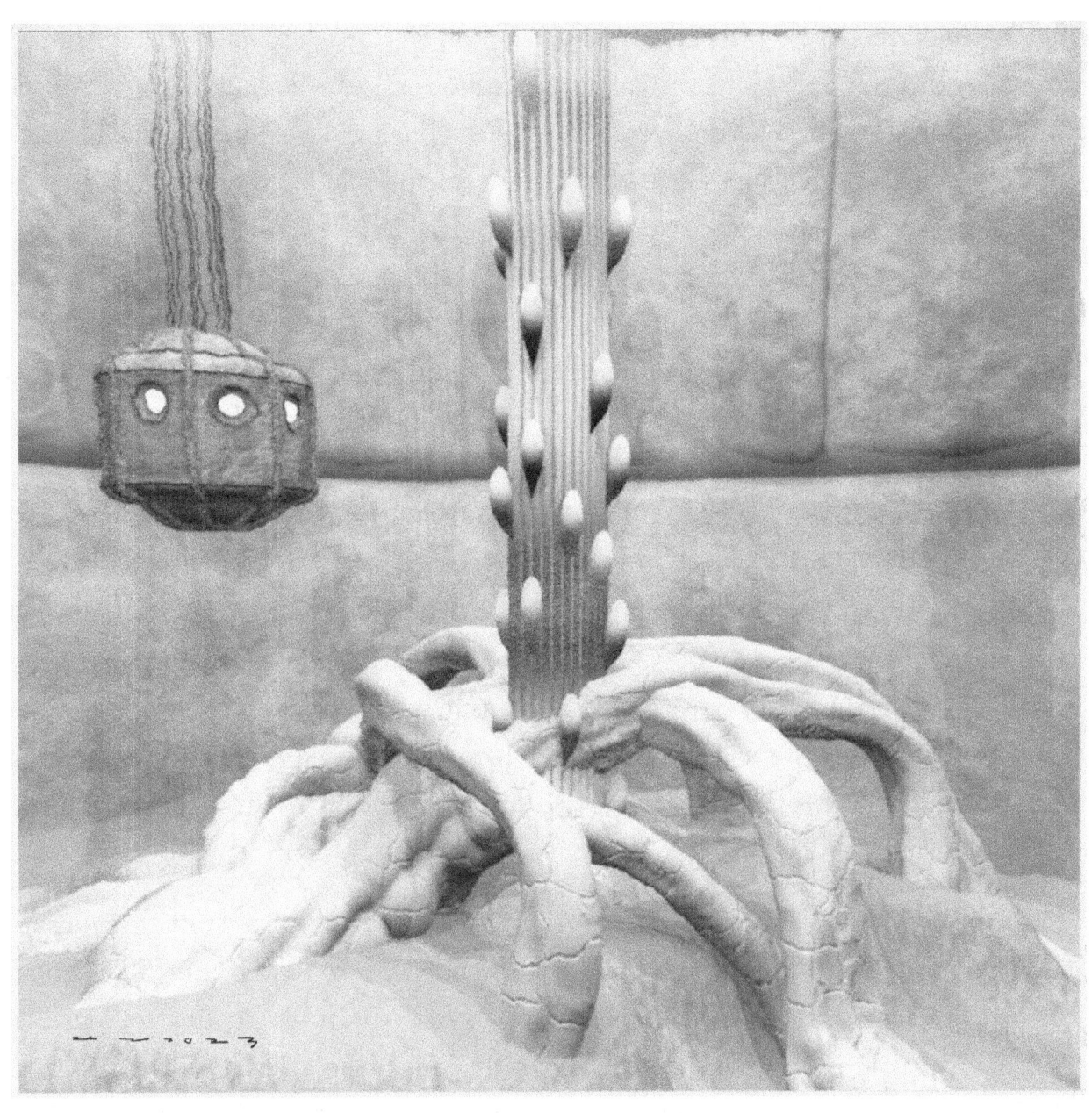

57. **AS THEY REACHED THE BOTTOM** of the tower core, the outside temperature was 887°F [410°C] and the pressure was 93 atmospheres.

Later, outside on the roof of the tower, Delos was equally amazed at the simulated Venus environment as much as he was with the furnace kelp. Terra declined to say how he managed to keep the pressures and temperatures separated in the tower's core, only that it enabled him to create a miniature version of a plant that would work in the Venusian atmosphere. Terra had setbacks during development when for no reason a tankless atmosphere would suddenly collapse, and he would have to start over. He was just glad there wasn't an incident during Delos's visit. It was just as Dana warned earlier, Terra thought to himself. Delos tried to press for information but got nowhere. He felt Terra's development of the atmospheric simulation may be just as much or even more valuable than his creation of furnace kelp. It was clear to Delos that with seeming indifference, Terra had created (at least in part) what was long sought after by anyone who dreamed of life beyond Earth; an artificial atmospheric field. It was an artificial condition that allowed for a habitable micro-climate to exist where none should exist at all. Delos began to wonder about the possibilities of this new discovery and how it could change off-world settlements everywhere. Delos felt he could reopen Elysium Donte if it was under an artificial atmosphere. He knew somehow, he had to learn Terra's secret. Perhaps in time Terra would reveal clues. But for now, Delos knew he had to wait, at least until the furnace kelp was planted on Venus. For the next phase of the plan Terra would begin producing furnace kelp seeds, thousands of them.

On June 10th, 1920 (4 years and 3 months since Delos saw the first miniature furnace kelp) thousands of unmanned drones descended from space into the upper atmosphere across the face of Venus. From the viewpoint of the floating settlements, their arrival was like a grand meteor storm that filled the skies in every direction. Having slowed down from re-entry, the drones flew down to an altitude of 40 miles [64.3 kilometers]. From that altitude each released thousands of furnace kelp seeds before running out of fuel and plunging down to the surface below. The heat and pressure of the troposphere was so intense the drones broke up in flight and only small bits of metal rained down the surface below. June 10th officially marked the beginning of the terraforming of Venus. Flying alongside some of the drones Delos and Terra watched as the planet was seeded with life.

58. **HUNDREDS OF PILOTLESS CRAFT** descend into the upper atmosphere of Venus releasing thousands of seeds prior to running out of fuel and plunging into the furnace below.

59. WHILE TERRA WAS ON VENUS overseeing the planting of furnace kelp, something unusual happened in a forgotten part of his greenhouse on Eden Island. The sealed chamber that was once used to grow the first furnace kelp still contained Venusian soil. It was soil Terra once handled with his bare hands. Unknown to Terra, a perfect bust of his head formed out of the soil.

June 10ᵗʰ, 1922, exactly two years after the furnace kelp was planted, an estimated 83% of the seeds had successfully taken root. Each had grown into a hill approximately 100 feet [30.4 meters] high with a footprint of 300 feet [91.4 meters] in diameter. After the planting, Terra began making annual trips to Venus to check on the progress of his creation. Delos was pleased at Terra's work and felt he had accomplished his goal even though the furnace kelp was still in its infancy.

60. **MECHINICAL WORKERS FROM ELYSIUM DONTE** inspect the early rise of furnace kelp. Thousands of kelp roots were beginning to grow all across the planet. The terraforming of Venus atmosphere had begun.

61. **1923, JOHN POWERS TERRA (4ᵗʰ)** was born in the greenhouse on Avalon Island.

By 1923 the average height of furnace kelp was 600 feet [182.9 meters]. James Powers Terra (3rd) came to the end of his life segment. In his last hour he went to the Green House on Avalon Island and surrendered his memories to John Powers Terra (4th). Like the others before, John would continue almost exactly where his predecessor left off. To the public he was nephew to his late uncle and sole heir to his estate. Less than a year later he announced he was taking over his uncle's affairs.

Unknown to anyone, Terra had re-engineered the life regeneration process for himself. To everyone in the immortal's club, regeneration was done by simply laying on a lunar mushroom pad, falling asleep then waking up in a new body. After going before the shadows, Terra began to fear for his life, so he developed a way to regenerate in the event he was murdered before returning home. He developed a pod plant that would grow a new body by itself. To pass his memories on at the end of a life cycle, Terra would simply rest his head in one of the pod's open flowers. After doing so, he would fall asleep, and his memories would transfer to the new body growing in the pod. As an extra precaution, Terra kept an active journal. In the event that he was killed before passing on his memories, the new Terra could access the journal after he was born. John Powers Terra (the 4th of his kind) was born with 217 years of memories.

On a dark evening in July 1924 three parties of six men each invaded Eden Island while Terra was on Venus overseeing the progress of furnace kelp. The first group approached by sea. Less than a mile offshore their boat was snagged by a plant, pulled under and they were never seen again. The second party was dropped in the center of the island by parachute.

They broke into one of Terra's labs and tried to photograph as many documents as they could before coming under attack. One by one something unseen pulled each of them away from the group into the surrounding darkness. The last survivor of the second group managed to make it down to the Tower of Venus near the shore to contact the third party that also parachuted in. By that time the third group managed to steal one of the small metal sphere devices that was used to recreate the artificial atmosphere in the tower. A short time later they were all killed, but not before attaching the stolen items and camera to a balloon and releasing it. When Terra returned to Eden and saw that someone tried to invade the island, he wasn't surprised. Over the years there had been several attempts to learn his secrets at any cost. No uninvited visitors ever returned.

62. **THE LAST SURVIVOR** of the three teams that invaded Eden Island managed to attach stolen items to a balloon before being killed. Terra wasn't surprised when he heard of the event. No uninvited visitors to Eden Island have ever survived. Unknown to Terra, the invaders were sent by Delos.

In 1930 it came as no surprise to Terra when he received a request from Delos to come to Gilgamesh Island. He last regenerated in 1880 which meant his 50-year life cycle was about to end. In his message Delos reported he was now 70 and in poor health due to exposure to the sun's rays from time spent on Venus. He wanted to regenerate.

Alex Cristos Delos (2nd) arrived at Gilgamesh Island on August 7th. Terra wasted no time in getting everything ready. Everything went as planned. Delos entered the re-generation chamber alone, laid on the mat and quickly fell asleep. Later he awoke in a new body with only the skeleton of his former body on top of him. He brushed it aside, got up and dressed. His new body was approximately 24 years old. The re-generation was normal, but Terra was surprised to see that Delos was now a younger version of his reconstructed self, not his original self. Delos explained his reconstruction was done on a gene level. His very makeup had been altered. It was the only way to save his life. Terra understood it but it also seemed strange that Delos would have so many bodyguards. This time they kept his skeleton. It seemed curious to Terra, but he later dismissed it. Considering what was happening on Venus, Delos might have made some enemies, but then for most people in his position, having enemies was not uncommon. After regeneration he became Alex Manson Delos (3rd) and followed the narrative that he was sole heir to his uncle's estate. That same year Terra's friend Margret Dana also regenerated. Nancy Anna Dana (2nd) became Marie Anna Dana (3rd).

By 1935 the average furnace kelp height was now just over three miles [four point eight kilometers]. They were growing at an astonishing rate. Terra was pleased with their progress. Even though they were only a minimal fraction of their mature height, they had already begun to break down sulfuric acid in the atmosphere. The effect was almost negligible, but things were moving in the right direction. All over Venus the grand stalks of furnace kelp ascending into the thick brown clouds above were a common sight. The surface pressure had dropped to 85 atmospheres.

63. 1935, **A HOVER FALCON** with Terra on board, flies down in the lower atmosphere of Venus for a short time as he inspects the growing furnace kelp.

By 1940 Delos was able to make progress with the information recovered from the Tower of Venus break-in years earlier. From the recovered material Delos concluded the conditions in the tower had been created with the application of Merlin's SEE energy. Very quietly and secretly Delos and his right-hand man on Venus, Alberto Santos, oversaw their own experiments in an attempt to recreate, at least in part, a tankless atmosphere.

64. **AFTER YEARS OF TRIAL AND ERROR,** Delos and Santos were able to recreate a tankless atmosphere from the material stolen from Eden Island years earlier.

After years of trial-and-error Delos and Santos successfully created their own miniature atmosphere over Elysium Donte. Inside the area, the pressure was 1.2 Earth atmospheres, the temperature was down to 143°F [62°C], and the air was almost breathable. The artificial envelope was powered by the heat of the outside atmosphere. With this new development, Delos decided to reopen Elysium Donte.

65. BY 1940 ELYSIUM DONTE reopened under the tankless atmosphere.

The venture to reopen Elysium Donte was a real gamble. Even if successful, it wouldn't pay off for another 160 years, not until Venus was terraformed. Delos's plan was to mine the ore, and process it into raw material, but the real problem was protecting it from the harsh atmosphere. If his plan worked, Delos would have the materials there on hand when it came time to build the roads and cities that would eventually populate Venus.

That same year, the Venus space station project was passed by the world powers back on Earth. They believed it would serve as a gateway to Venus during the terraforming period. Delos was able to secure a contract to provide some of the building materials necessary for the station. To that end, half of the Delos prison facility was to be reconfigured to an industrial section capable of fabricating some of the station components. The cable between Delos and Elysium Donte was replaced with one that could support a grand elevator. Recently new kinds of materials existed where their molecules were interlocked, increasing their strength properties to a level only dreamed of before. Delos was one of the first to make use of it on a grand scale. This new material made a suspended cable elevator between Delos and Elysium Donte possible.

Very few grand elevators existed. (A grand elevator is defined as one that can travel from the ground to high altitudes in the upper atmosphere.) Delos christened his elevator "Ascensor Darvaza". It was as tall as a six-story building. Yet, despite its size and carrying capacity it could bring only limited amounts of ore up to Delos. To make the most efficient use of the elevator, Delos decided it should only carry refined material. This meant constructing mills at Elysium Donte to refine the ore from its mines. When word of the Venus elevator first became public, news reporters were eager to see the accomplishment up close. Delos declined any attempt. When asked if Elysium Donte was going to be another prison, Delos responded it was maintained by mechanical workers who were conducting studies on preparation for the terraforming of Venus and mining raw material to build the space station. The furnace kelp now had an average height of six miles [nine point seven kilometers].

66. **THE ASCENSOR DARVAZA** begins its 43-mile [69.2 kilometers] descent to the Elysium Donte. The cable spools are covered in a glass ceramic to reduce the effect of acid rain. The elevator itself consists of two large chambers, with 16-foot [4.9 meter] ceilings, stacked one over the other. The overall length of the elevator is 120 feet [36.5 meters] and is supported by 3 nano flex ceramic cables.

In the years that followed, it was clear to Delos with the tankless atmosphere (TLA) in place, his mining settlement, Elysium Donte could grow. One of the interesting side effects of TLA was it also blocked any electronic surveillance. Delos noticed it while reviewing electronic images of Elysium Donte taken from above. The area where the settlement below should be, was blocked out. Fearing that others observing the area might see the same thing and become curious, Delos had several balloons anchored in and around Elysium Donte with transmitters that would produce a false image, making any electronic surveillance of the area appear normal. As the settlement expanded, Delos knew he would have to set up more transmitters.

The furnace Kelp was growing and working as planned. The temperature and pressure at the equator were now 835°F [446°C], 83 atmospheres. It was down by 28°F, 9 atmospheres, but according to Terra, progress would be very slow in the early years of change. Delos was now beginning to have thoughts of his Venus plan's third phase. He knew one way or another, the planet would eventually become another Earth. But he also knew there would be a long period of transition when it would be hybrid of both Earth and Venus. That meant even after some areas became cool enough for habitation, others would still be far too hostile for people to live.

As part of his plan, Delos had several off-world prisons. Security was easy to maintain in environments harmful to life. It also meant in settlements "out on the frontier" (as it was referred to on Earth), the administrators could do pretty much whatever they wanted. Early on Delos knew his floating penal colony would become a source of opportunity if Venus could be terraformed. For some time, he was fascinated with the possibility of conducting hybrid life experiments involving the use of the re-generation process. One of the older and more mysterious members of the shadows, Dr. Serco, gave Delos the initial idea during a visit Delos made to the Black Castle. For several years Delos wondered about the possibilities of creating and controlling a hybrid sub-humanoid race that was better adapted to the Venusian environment. He felt they could become a surface taskforce that could start development when it was still far too dangerous for people. Also, if necessary, they would make a powerful army when needed. And his source for this new hybrid race was naturally, the prisoners. For them life was almost hopeless. He felt the opportunity to start over on a new planet might appeal to some of them. As he looked out over the cloud tops of Venus from his chamber, Delos believed in Milton's classic expression "It was better to rule in Hell than serve in Heaven". With that thought in mind he quietly began to draw his plans for creating a sub-human task force.

The initial idea for creating a sub-human race came to Delos when Dr. Serco told the story of an unsuccessful re-generation that had gone bad. Delos already knew if anything else was present in the re-generation chamber (even the smallest insect) it would become part of the individual forming into a new hybrid life form. It was then that Delos learned Terra wasn't the only one who had perfected the process of regeneration. Dr. Serco had also perfected the process. Delos was somewhat frightened by what Dr. Serco told him next. He said that he had overseen sub-human hybrid experiments of combining animals to form completely new life forms. Dr. Serco told him of a hidden island not far off the coast of England. It was where his experiments took place. Serco laughed when he said many creatures on his island could be found in the fantasies of English folklore. Delos had the feeling he was dealing with a monster. Then again, he felt this could be a useful monster if it meant achieving his goals.

Dr. Serco seemed to be a well-informed man. Delos wondered if Serco knew of the clandestine efforts he had made so far in an effort to perfect the regeneration process on his own. The pads made from the skin of giant lunar mushrooms were extremely hard to come by. Terra only allowed re-generation under his close supervision. Years ago, back in March 1936 Delos seized a shipment of lunar mushrooms bound for Earth and made it look as though the ship had been lost in space. Later in a secret lab at Delos Prison he was able, at least in part, to reproduce the same effect of the pads Terra had created.

67. DR. SERCO GAVE DELOS the initial idea of creating a sub-human race on Venus during a visit Delos made to the Black Castle.

Delos told Serco he had thousands of lunar pads, more than enough to convert all the prisoners. He told him his team on Venus had been working in secret and were continuing to experiment. Serco told Delos he need not work any further, he had developed a tissue sample that will create the desired result. He had already developed a powerful sub-humanoid creature. At that moment, Dr. Serco pulled out a small, sealed vial containing a tissue sample and gave it to Delos. The question before Delos now was "Who would be the first?"

When Delos returned to Venus with the sample, he was surprised that his right-hand man Alberto Santos volunteered to be the first. Santos had been assisting Delos for years and knew fully well what he was getting into. Since Delos prison was first established back in 1895, Alberto Santos ran the facility. For many years Santos had been one of his most loyal employees, so much so that without him running the prison might not have been possible. After Santos went through the transformation, he became more physically powerful than anyone imagined. The prisoner's respect and fear for him increased many times. It was March 1941.

Santos was the approximate size of a man, but he had an enormous appetite. Seemingly overnight he started growing at a rapid rate. His weight got up to 550 pounds and had reached a height of 8 feet [2.43 meters] three weeks later. Born in 1870, Alberto Jorge Santos (1st) was 71 years old before re-generating. After going through the procedure, he changed his name to Milton Jorge Santos (2nd). Because he was no longer human there was far less reason for changing his name, but he did it just the same.

Santos was the first of his kind. He also had 20 guards under him who were extremely loyal. To follow him they also volunteered to change their form. Santos suggested it would be wise to transform them before approaching the prison population. Delos agreed and by April 1941, the transformed men numbered 21.

68. ALBERTO SANTOS was the first of his kind. He stopped growing after reaching a height of eight feet [two point four meters] and had the strength of 10 to 12 men.

Because Santos and the transformed guards reminded Delos of creatures out of a fantasy novel, he called them orcs. They were just right for his purpose. Delos would rule them and ultimately, they would rule Venus. Like Santos, they grew to be the same weight and height. Their skin was like leathery armor plating that could easily resist small arms fire. They also had higher resistance to heat. They could withstand temperatures up to +200°F [93°C], that made them suitable for work in the mines of Elysium Donte with minimal life support. But Delos knew such a group, even a small group could easily take over the prison.

Delos wanted Elysium Donte to ultimately become an orc colony. He knew for his new race of orcs to be effective they had to increase their numbers. By now Elysium Donte had many large underground caverns that had been abandoned as the mining moved on. With preserved mushrooms brought back from Earth's Moon, Delos started his own subterranean lunar garden on Venus. Once established, he could grow his own regeneration pads and greatly increase the orc population.

Being a strong motivational speaker had always been a requirement for a corporate leader. For Delos it would be a tough sell persuading the prisoners to become orcs to help develop Venus. His speech under the guise about building an empire turned out to be more successful than he had hoped. By early 1960 the orcs numbered 1347, and nearly all the guards had been transformed. To the outside world Elysium Donte was a small settlement where soil samples had been collected by mechanical workers. To Delos it was now a thriving orc settlement under his tight control. However, even to the orcs it was a hellish place. They often referred to the cable transport as the "Elevator to Hell". By now all the mechanical workers had been replaced by orcs. To keep their population growing at a steady rate Delos had more and more prisoners transferred to Venus from his other off-world facilities, and eventually Elysium Donte. Once at Elysium Donte they were highly motivated to become orcs. If they didn't get transformed, they became slaves and on occasion a meal for the orcs. By now the equatorial temperature was 788°F [420°C] and the pressure was 78.2 atmospheres. The average height of furnace kelp was now 13 miles [20.9 kilometers].

After 20 years of planning, the primary base module for the new Venera space station arrived from Earth and construction began. By 1970 Elysium Donte was also the home of the largest mushroom forest off the Moon.

69. **THE GRAND LUNAR MUSHROOM FOREST** of Elysium Donte.

70. **IN 1973 JOHN POWERS TERRA** (4TH) came to the end of his life segment. He went to the greenhouse and surrendered his memories to his successor Paul Powers Terra (5TH). Terra continued to make periodic trips to Venus to oversee the progress of his furnace kelp.

By 1980 the equatorial temperature on Venus was 738°F [392°C)], down by almost 47°F, and the pressure was now 73 atmospheres. Venus was changing. Back on Earth there had already been fraudulent Venus real estate swindles. Almost since the year it reopened back in 1940, Delos delegated control of Elysium Donte to his strong man Milton Santos, who had been the leader of the orcs since their inception.

By now the orcs were beginning to show signs of their own culture, reflected in the architecture of their stone buildings with horn-like features. During his visits to Elysium Donte, Delos began to wonder about the formula that was used to produce the orcs in the first place. Even though Dr. Serco told him it was a special mix of animal tissue, the orc culture suggested it carried a gene of some lost intelligence, or lost species that had its own culture. For a brief moment Delos thought there might be some truth to the fantasy stories surrounding orcs. By now the orcs had established smaller outpost settlements away from Elysium Donte. It was risky. As before, sometimes the tankless atmosphere would suddenly collapse and because there was no place to retreat to, the outpost and everyone in it would fry in an instant. The orc population was now 50,000. Another step toward self-reliance was food production. As mining progressed over the years several large underground cavern networks were discovered. In an effort to increase the settlements habitable areas, Delos had the caverns sealed off, depressurized and the temperature lowered to match the TLA atmosphere. The average height of furnace kelp was now 30 miles. The Venera space station was half complete. Thirty seven percent of the station's structure was made using materials mined from Elysium Donte.

As early as 1981, Delos realized that any kind of attempt at food production in the mining caverns would fall short of what was required to feed the growing orc population. There had been rumors surrounding the large food shipments to the Delos prison on Venus, considering it had a reduced prison population. To satisfy food demand, the orcs needed something beyond conventional food.

71. BY 1981 ELYSIUM DONTE had become an Orc colony and they were beginning to show signs of their own culture, reflected in the architecture of their stone buildings with horn-like features.

To overcome the food problem, Milton suggested to Delos introducing the lunar octovine to the caverns of Elysium Donte. The dangerous fast-growing plant known as the Octovine in lunar caves was well known. It got its name because its vines were much like the tentacles of an Octopus. One of the things that made it so deadly was it was in some ways like an animal that hunted its prey, and it had a taste for humans. It grew and traveled only in a remote stretch of the lunar Amazon cavern.

Having traveled to the Moon years earlier, it was Milton who first suggested growing it on Venus. Unlike humans, the orcs were powerful creatures. What might be dangerous to humans could be a food source for orcs. Delos liked the Idea. The lunar mushrooms had been successfully growing in the caves for years. Perhaps it was time to cultivate another lunar plant. In October 1981 Delos managed to smuggle five plants off the Moon. By March of 1982, they were planted at Elysium Donte in a remote area. They thrived and as Milton predicted. They became a suitable food source for the orcs. In addition, they became added security against any unwelcome visitors.

Other than an official press release from Delos, there was very little correspondence coming from Venus about the surface settlement of Elysium Donte. Some of the prisoner's families were beginning to wonder why so many inmates in off-world prisons controlled by Delos were being transferred to Venus. It was known the Delos prison had been reduced to make room for a manufacturing facility to produce space station components. This prompted well-known independent news correspondent Jeffery Donald to pursue the story. The outside world believed Elysium Donte had a population that consisted mostly of mechanical workers. Yet early on, Donald discovered several companies involved with mechanical workers had no orders from Delos for many years. In his research, Donald also discovered food shipments to the Delos prison on Venus had increased by ten times since 1945 and yet there was no increase in the prison population that anyone knew of.

72. UNKNOWN TO THE OUTSIDE WORLD, octovines from the Moon had been on Terra's lands for many years. He used them to protect his islands. They had been altered to attack and consume only uninvited visitors.

Upon request Donald was granted a visit to Delos, but after arriving he was kept in an area near the landing pads and wasn't allowed to see any of the prisoners. He was told there had been an outbreak and the isolation was for his own safety. And he wasn't allowed anywhere near the cable elevator. After two days of frustration, he left Delos only to return later concealed inside a food shipment being transferred from orbit. Not knowing what he would be exposed to, Donald wore a long duration space suit. He was somewhat shocked that the container was filled with frozen dead horses and cattle. After his container arrived at the Delos loading area, all became quiet. Donald emerged from the container. He opened his helmet to hear better. Moving in the shadows he heard two guards talking about the next container bound for Elysium Donte. After they left, Donald climbed back into the container. At first, he thought of being roasted in the lower atmosphere, but he was reassured by the fact that he was riding in a food shipment. There was the usual jostling as his container was loaded into the cable elevator.

The slow descent came and seemed to go on forever. At first there was the faint sound of wind, typical for floating cities like Delos. But as the minutes passed it blew stronger and stronger. Then Donald could hear the distant sound of thunder. It grew louder and louder until it was almost deafening. The elevator began to rock violently. Then the thunder began to fade, and it was calm once more. The sound of rain followed. There was also a sizzling sound as the rain hit the elevator outside. Donald knew it was raining sulfuric acid, but it would end at they got lower. Another hour passed. Donald was suddenly overcome with a strange sensation. It was as though he passed through some sort of barrier. A few minutes later, the elevator finally came to rest. He was now on the surface of Venus. There was more movement as his container was unloaded.

73. **THE ASCENSOR DARVAZA** departs from Delos Prison with news correspondent Jeffery Donald hiding in a food container.

Donald's food container was somewhere inside Elysium Donte. Through his helmet he could hear the faint sounds of guards talking as they counted the number of containers. Their voices seemed unusually deep. He heard them leaving. Then it was quiet. Slowly and quietly, Donald emerged from the container. After removing his helmet, he was almost overcome by the heat and the intense smell of the rotting animal corpses in the containers all around him. His suit indicated 131°F [55°C]. "How can anyone work in this?" he thought to himself. He adjusted his suit temperature to compensate. Moving quietly, he made his way into one of the corridors that led away from the area. At the end of it was a large iron door. Donald could hear a faint conversation coming from the other side. It was a guard talking to one of the prisoners. The prisoner was telling the guard how good it was to be away from Delos where he could work. Soon the guard left.

Donald felt if he could speak to one of the prisoners, he could get some answers. He pulled the side lever to open the doors. The iron doors slowly opened. Donald was wrong. It wasn't the prisoner; it was the guard. Donald looked up in horror and stumbled back at the site of the huge orc in front of him. "My God! It's some sort of monster" he thought as he dropped his helmet, too shocked to speak. Before he could react, the guard was upon him, picked him up, turned around and threw him into an octovine plant field nearby. The plants quickly devoured Donald. Even his suit was consumed, but later one of the plants belched out his helmet and breathing apparatuses.

74. DONALD LOOKED UP IN HORROR and stumbled back at the site of the

huge orc.

As the years passed, James Powers Terra (4th) became Paul Powers Terra (5th) in 1973. Marie Anna Dana (3rd) regenerated and became Marriana Anna Dana (4th) in 1980. That same year Alex Manson Delos (3rd) became Alex Bester Delos (4th). In 1991 Milton regenerated. There was no need to change his name because aside from Delos, Dr. Serco, and a handful of others, he has no direct contact with humans.

By the year 2000 the rotation of a day on Venus had stabilized at 23 hours and 57 minutes. The equatorial surface temperature was now 676°F [358°C], a drop of 187°F since the furnace kelp was first planted. Surface pressure was now 68 atmospheres. The average kelp height was now 45 miles [72.4 kilometers]. At some of the higher areas on the furnace kelp, algae islands were beginning to form to start the process of converting carbon dioxide into oxygen. The algae islands of furnace kelp (as they came to be called) would become a temporary place where surface settlements would be possible, but only for a century or two. They were a fundamental part of the terraforming process and Terra knew many of them would become inhabited, if only for a few years. The first settlers were mostly scientists who specialized in meteorology and monitored the growth and health of the furnace kelp. They were housed in temporary yurts that were set up on the kelp all over Venus.

75. BY 2000 THE ALGAE ISLANDS of furnace kelp had become large enough to land on. Temporary yurts were put in place on many of them. Even though the atmospheric air-pressure and temperature were close to that of Earth, protection was still required for resistance against sulfuric acid.

Delos knew when Venus had a cooler, breathable atmosphere, millions of people would come. He felt many would come even sooner with just the promise that Venus would become a second Earth. Even though there was little change in atmospheric temperature and pressure, more surface settlements were beginning to appear on Venus. They were small and mainly for the purpose of establishing land claims. At the present rate of change, the planetary transformation was less than two centuries away.

In the years that followed the re-creation of the tankless atmosphere (TLA), made the re-habitation of Elysium Donte possible. The Delos team developed a smaller portable version that could be used on a vehicle. Delos wanted to do a closer observation of Venus to expand his mining interests. With that in mind he commissioned an exploration airship to be built that would carry its own TLA on board. It would be constructed at the newly completed service facility at Elysium Donte. An airship having a TLA on board was nothing new, but no one was aware that Delos had access to it. The TLA would keep the ship in a cool, low-pressure environment wherever it traveled and block any electronic detection from above. The constant cloud cover of Venus would conceal it completely. This ship would allow Delos to explore the continents of Venus up close long before anyone else. In addition to the TLA, the new ship would also be equipped with a ground penetrating sensor to search for the existence of any underground caverns that might be suitable for future mining and possible settlements. In 2002 the ship was completed. It was christened Pluto One. With a crew of 20 orcs, it began a series of long voyages exploring the vast unknown horizons of Venus. Less than 3 years later, Delos had a small fleet of 21 ships roaming the surface of Venus. Three were lost when their TLA's failed.

76. **IN 2002 DELOS COMMISSIONED AIRSHIPS** equipped with their own tankless atmospheres to survey the surface of Venus for precious minerals and sites for possible underground settlements. The first of these survey ships was the Pluto One airship.

77. UNKNOWN TO DELOS, Dr. Serco had a direct liaison with Milton. Milton knew Serco had provided the flesh that converted the humans into orcs. After going through the regeneration process, Milton and the other orcs started having feelings and memories of being on a dry yellow planet. Serco suggested adding live animals to the cave network. He also told Milton of a vast cave network located approximately 5000 miles [8046.8 kilometers] directly southeast of Elysium Donte.

Milton directed one of the pluto airships to survey the area south that Serco spoke of. The cave network was discovered. It turned out to be much larger than Milton imagined. They were the deepest caves discovered so far and were 20 times the size of those below Elysium Donte. At the suggestion of Serco, Milton christened the cave network Mare Caverna. The caves were sealed off, cooled, and depressurized to 1.2 atmospheres by 2008. The cave network was like a star that had a large center cavity with grand underground tributaries stretching out for miles in all directions. The network was rich in mineral deposits. Milton reported the discovery to Delos but made no mention of his association with Serco.

There was no explanation why this happened or what caused it. In the year 2010, two years after the orcs moved into Mare Caverna, water began seeping into the caves. Up to that point, no subterranean water was thought to exist anywhere on Venus. The water kept rising until a lake formed in the central area with river waterways extending out in all directions. It also caused an island to form in the central area. At that point it stopped rising. The cave water was cold and clear. This made the caves ideal for expanding the orc race. Milton knew he could not oversee both Mare Caverna and Elysium Donte at the same time, so he selected a trusted orc lieutenant, Rubin, and put him in charge. Rubin was once a prisoner who was loyal to both Delos and Milton (back when Milton was Santos).

By 2015 the island in Mare Caverna's central area became the location of Caverna City, the capital of Mare Caverna. Rubin had a throne room built just for him. Both Delos and Milton were pleased at the progress Rubin was making. The orc population was growing at a steady pace. Delos was hoping to get his future army in place. Milton was hoping to be able to rule the orcs independent of humans. Less than two years later Stratus (the twin city to Delos) had been established and was floating over Mare Caverna with two elevators in place.

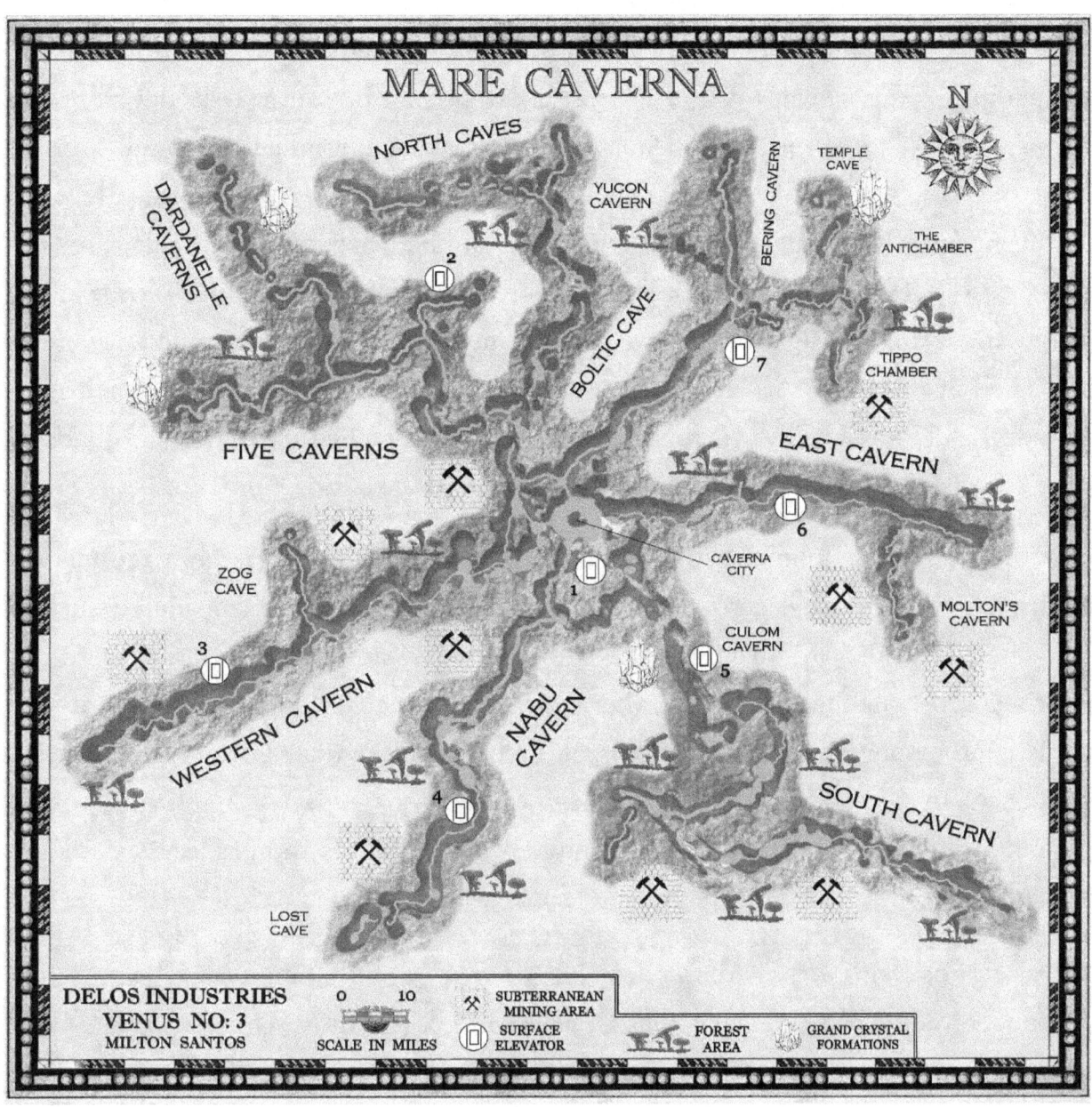

78. THE GRAND CAVE NETWORK of Mare Caverna, Venus. The water rose enough to cut off some of the outer tunnels. To reestablish connections, submarines large enough for orcs were constructed. The caves also gave rise to a unique ecosystem with the orcs at the top of the food chain.

By 2020 the furnace kelp was fully grown. It grew much faster than anyone expected. Even Terra had trouble trying to figure out the cause. The kelp's average height was now approximately 67 miles [108 kilometers]. At the equator the temperature was down to 609°F [321°C] and the pressure was down to 63 atmospheres. The orc population was now 100,000 at Elysium Donte and 8000 at Mare Caverna. It wasn't long until small human settlements were established high up in the furnace kelp's algae islands where the air had become breathable, and the pressure and temperature were becoming more suitable for human life. Terra warned against it, saying the algae islands were only temporary and would crumble when the kelp died at the end of its life. But no one listened and the settlements grew. As a precaution, Terra and Dana arranged to have TLA's installed on the algae islands to protect against the lingering effects of sulfuric acid in the atmosphere.

In the years that followed, thousands of these settlements on the algae islands continued to pop up all across Venus. Although they were not considered surface settlements, the kelp villages were the first open human settlements that were not floating. Most all the villages on the algae islands had "Kelp" somewhere in the settlement name. Not far from Delos at Kelp Chandra, Pual Powers Terra had a residence. In 2023 when his life segment came to an end, Terra returned to the greenhouse on Avalon Island and surrendered his memories to his successor George Powers Terra.

It was 2030. Delos was at the end of his 50-year regeneration cycle. As expected, Terra received word from Delos that he wanted to regenerate. While Delos had been creating and regenerating orcs on a grand scale, he never trusted the pads to use on himself. Like Terra and the others in the Immortals Club, Delos had a similar cover story for the public as he would fake his own death, alter his appearance, and start a new identity as a relative who was the sole heir to the fortune. The mining and development of Elysium Donte continued to be successful. Since 2014 there had been three elevators operating between there and Delos.

79. **BY 2020, FULLY GROWN FURNACE KELP** had an average height of 67 miles [108 kilometers].

80. **AFTER LANDING ON FURNACE KELP**, Terra steps out for a closer inspection.

81. A TYPICAL ALGAE ISLAND SETTLEMENT grew without regard to the fact that the algae islands on furnace kelp were only temporary. Even though the air pressure and temperature were comparable to Earth, every algae island had a TLA to protect against the lingering amount of sulfuric acid in the atmosphere.

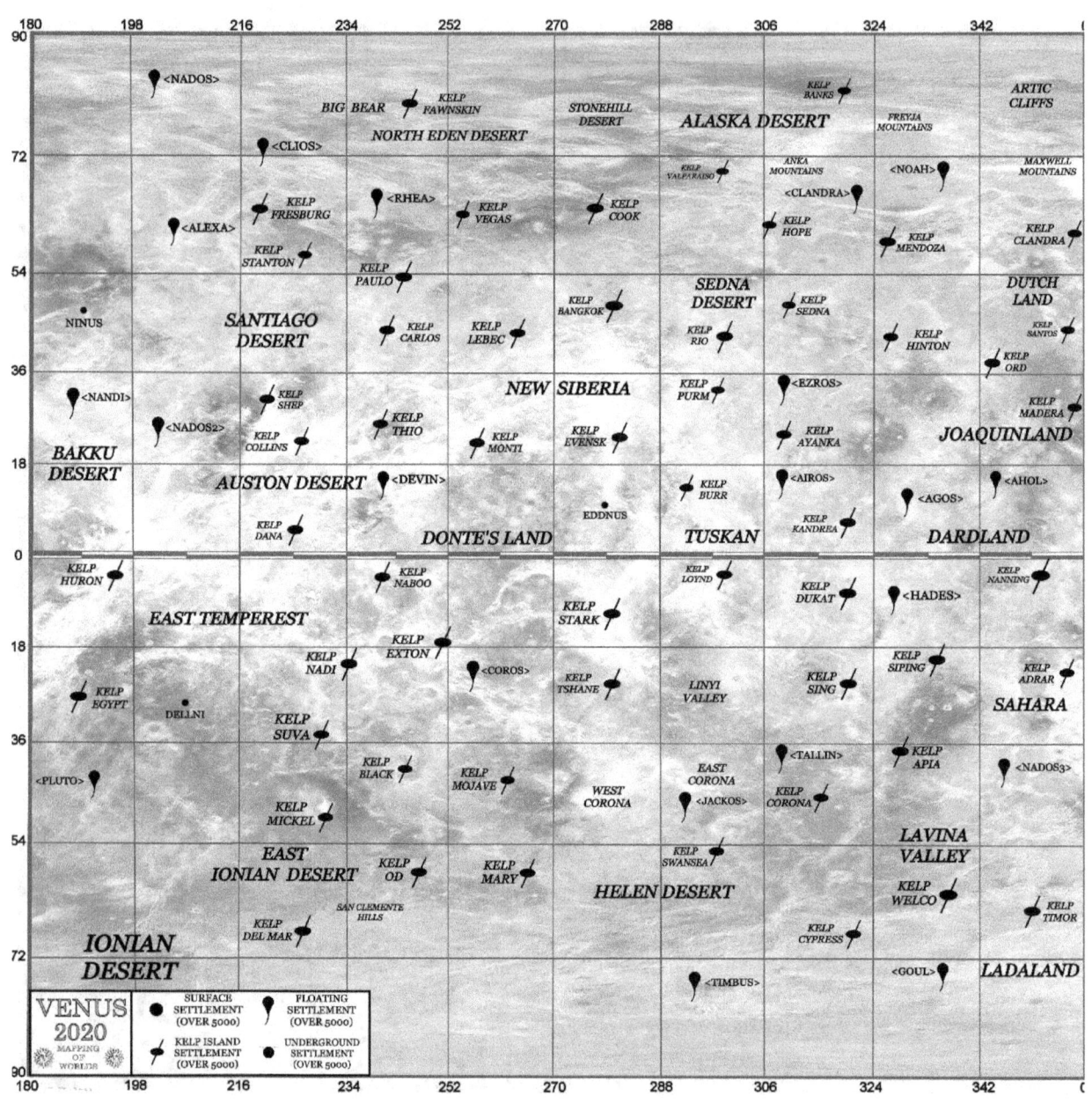

82. A MAP OF VENUS SETTLEMENTS by the year 2020. Even though the terraforming of Venus was well under way, only two percent of population lived on the surface. [Surface image by NASA]

NORTH VALLEY

MESA DESERT

NORTH YALLEY

<FADIN>

KELP KEROS   <ALINA>   KELP POLAR

<DELOS>
ELYSIUM DONTE

EAST TERRA

KELP LOWEL   KELP DENVER   AUDRA YALLEY   KELP ISTANBUL   KELP ATHENS   <RENOS>   KELP KONA

<SIRRUS>   <TAVOS>   <MILOS>   KELP ROA

KELP PERAK

KELP DEVIN   KELP FRESNO   KELP MILDURA   KELP DARWIN   KELP NANTOU

SANDERS MOUNTAIN   KELP PERTH   <GEORGA>   <EVEOS>   <AZRA>   KELP BREDA   LANKA HILLS

<STRATUS>
MARE CAVERNA   KELP NEPTUNE   CRITON   KELP HAWKER   NIOBE VALLEY   KELP SUBU   <WORDLAND>   KELP NASSER   KELP WELLINGTON

KELP VENUS   KELP TROY   KELP ACCRA   KELP RERALI   <VEROS>

KELP ACRON   MALAYSIA DESERT   <MOUL>

STEAMLAND
<CUMULUS>   KELP NORCO   KELP CAIRO   WEST TERRA   KELP CADIZ   KELP RABON   KELP KLAATU

KELP CYPRUS   RAGOON   KELP ROME   KELP ZAFRA

KELP MASON   KELP TANNIS   <BELOS>   KELP BORJA

KELP TUNIS   TANNUS   KELP LUXOR   KELP SIGUENZA

CORONO VALLEY   TEMPEREST DESERT   <ALARA>   ESPANA DESERT

NORTH MOROCCO   KELP OMAR   KELP MADRID

KELP MADEEN   CORONO DESERT   ARTENIS DESERT

SOUTH MOROCCO   KELP TANGIER   KELP KNOSSOS   KELP LANDER

BLANCA LAND   KELP NAVOI   TAMRON VALLEY   KELP MAIAYER   KELP ZAGORA

KELP MARRAKESH

KELP BALI   KELP UTAN   LEEDS DESERT   KELP EVERTON   KELP LEEDS   IONIAN DESERT

CONNUS

<MIMBUS>   LOSTLANDS   KELP PLYMOUTH   YORKSHIRE DESERT   <SOL>   KELP SATIE

<DINGUS>   KELP POLAR1   <ALTO>

KELP OTIS   DEVEN

EDEN DESERT

83. **WITHOUT REGARD TO TERRA'S** warning that the furnace kelp's algae islands were only temporary, island building was out of control. Even before the terraforming was finished, Venus became a new fronter for people who wanted to live off-world. While most of them knew they would never set foot in the surface, many believed Venus would be a place for their children and grandchildren.

84. **WHEN HE WAS ON VENUS,** Terra had a residence on Kelp Chandra near Delos and Elysium Donte.

In the year 2040, the orcs celebrated the 100th anniversary of their first home, Elysium Donte. The population was now 120,000. The equatorial temperature was now 542°F [283°C] (down by 315°F) and the pressure was now 59 atmospheres. The acid rain had finally stopped. For the better part of 20 years, human settlements were well established in the kelp algae islands high above. During that time there were several instances of shuttle crafts crashing and garbage being dumped in and around Elysium Donte and Mare Caverna. Most of it burned up. Milton found himself becoming less tolerant of humans over the years. He hoped the day would come when the orcs would no longer have any need for them. Every time something crashed or fell near the city, Milton was reminded of how much he wanted to rid them from the skies over Elysium Donte without drawing attention to the orcs. He finally solved his problem by releasing cannibal gnats from one of the cable elevators just before they reached Delos. One of the biggest problems for every off-world settlement was insects. Despite the best effort to sterilize space craft, they always managed to hitch a ride.

In the caves of Elysium Donte, the cannibal gnat (native to the Amazon area in lunar caves) came to Venus when Delos wanted to start a mushroom forest. Aside from being a tasty snack, they had little effect on the orcs, but to humans they were almost like a miniature flying piranha fish. The cannibal gnat is a small insect (approximately 4 inches [101.6 millimeters] in length) and flies around at the speed of a hummingbird. They proliferate in wet areas and feed on anything moist or what they think might be moist inside, including each other. Milton knew the kelp islands were filled with tide pools and small streams making them an ideal place for the gnats to populate. His plan worked. By early 2041 most all the kelp settlements above Elysium Donte had been abandoned. Six months later the settlements over Mare Caverna were also cleared out.

For the most part, the cannibal gnats were explained away, that is to all except George Terra. He believed their presence on Venus could indicate the possibility of lunar mushrooms being grown there by some clandestine group. Terra suspected someone working in Delos organization or possibly Delos himself. If it wasn't for the infestation's proximity to Delos and Stratus, Terra would have likely dismissed the idea. He knew once he started looking into the matter, his life would be in danger. From that point on he started to keep a detailed journal for his successor if he was killed before he could surrender his memories. Upon his next return to Venus, Terra's plan was to follow the trail.

Not long after his arrival on Venus, George Terra slowly descended through the upper cloud layer in his manta ray airship. He was 50 miles outside the outermost kelp settlement from Stratus where cannibal gnats had been reported. Even though the air pressure on the surface of Venus was down to 59 atmospheres and the temperature was down to 542°F [283°C], it still put a lot of stress on the airship's hull. The ship's only cabin was basically a life pod, but Terra wondered what the point was of being in a life pod when it was unlikely, he would be rescued if something went wrong. After an hour, Terra leveled off flying just 100 feet above the surface heading (unknowingly) straight for Mare Caverna. As he flew passed furnace kelp, he had the sensation he was flying through a dense forest in a deep yellow fog. He was now inside the area where the kelp settlements reported infestations. There was still no sign of anything unusual. Another hour passed. Stratus was straight ahead approximately 50 miles [80 kilometers] away.

A lone distant light down on the surface appeared ahead. Terra landed his ship nearby. He felt it was best to approach on foot from the shadows. As he got closer, he could see the light coming from a small pill box structure. There was no one around. Below the light was a single door. There was something else. According to Terra's handheld detector, the structure wasn't there. The detector indicated only open space. Still moving closer, he could make out a very faint transparent bubble around the structure. Approaching the door, he slowly stepped into the bubble. He felt a slight vibration in his hand as the detector started to react. The temperature suddenly dropped to 143°F [62°C] and the pressure dropped to 1.2 atmospheres. At that point Terra realized he was standing in a TLA. "So, this is where it ended up." Terra thought to himself. After his lab on Eden had been broken into 117 years ago back in 1924, he knew sooner or later the thieves might be able to recreate a TLA from the stolen material.

Terra opened the door by simply pushing on a pressure plate. "I guess out here there's no need for a lock of any kind", he thought as he stepped through. One thing that seemed odd was the size of the doors. They were large and looked more suitable for freight doors on a large warehouse. He passed through a small corridor and through a second set of doors. Terra stepped onto a metal cage that was suspended from the ceiling. It hung over a deep open shaft that had a faint light far below. It was an elevator. Once on the platform, it started to descend down a dark rocky shaft. The detector indicated the temperature dropped to 131°F [55°C] and the air had enough oxygen to make it breathable. He removed his helmet. The initial hot blast of air was overwhelming. The elevator descended out from the ceiling of a grand underground cavern. It was so large even Terra was somewhat overwhelmed by the sight of it. The cavern looked to be at least 250 to 300 feet [76.2 to 91.4 meters] high. But the real sight was the dense forest below that was illuminated by a greenish light beyond the bend at the far end of the cavern. It was almost like daylight.

85. **THE ELEVATOR DESCENDED** out from the ceiling of a grand underground cavern. It was so large even Terra was somewhat overwhelmed by the sight of it.

The elevator finally came to rest in an open area in the forest. It was absolutely quiet at first. Terra stepped out and was somewhat startled when the elevator behind him started to ascend back into the ceiling. He would have to find another way out. Terra slowly started to head toward the light at the far end of the grand chamber. He believed Delos was behind all of this and wondered how much more of his activities on Venus had been concealed from the outside world. Off in the distance he thought he saw birds flying low over the forest trees. As he got closer, he could see they were birds but not like any he had ever seen. They were prehistoric! They were small pterodactyls!

Terra heard something moving in the forest behind him. Whatever it was, the pterodactyls were attracted to it. They turned and started to fly in Terra's direction. At first, he feared for his life. A moment later when they flew past, they showed no interest in him at all. They dove into the forest behind. Terra could hear the sounds of an animal screaming and fighting as the pterodactyls attacked whatever was there. Seconds later they both flew up into the air pulling on the captured prey between them. It was a small dinosaur of some sort. It looked like a miniature raptor.

Outside, back on the surface, Terra's airship was spotted by an orc patrol ship. Still fearing for his life, Terra continued into the forest ahead. There was a small ridge overlooking the next cavern. Being careful to make sure there were no animals around Terra stepped out on the ridge. Below was a forest of lunar mushrooms, as far as the eye could see. As he looked out, he thought of what Delos was up to. He wondered if he was using the mushrooms to somehow recreate a prehistoric ecosystem to populate Venus when it became habitable. In an odd way Terra understood the reasoning behind creating and releasing prehistoric Earth life on Venus. It occurred to him that whenever he thought of dinosaurs in the past, the backdrop was always a much warmer Earth.

He heard the faint sound of something behind him. As Terra slowly turned around there were four orange dilophosaurus standing behind him. They were approximately 3 ½ to 4 feet high [1 to 1.2 meters]. He stood motionless as they approached. Judging by their teeth, Terra could see they could easily tear him to pieces in an instant. As they curiously circled around, each of them sniffed him up and down. Terra lost his fear when he realized they sensed only a plant and would not attack. That was why the pterodactyls didn't attack earlier. Three of the animals appeared to lose interest and ran off. The fourth one lifted his leg, urinated on his foot then ran off to join the others.

Still shaken by the encounter, Terra climbed down off the ridge and entered the mushroom forest. After hiking for several hours, he could hear the occasional sound and see a faint light of something sparking ahead. There was something different about this part of the cavern forest. It suddenly occurred to him that there were no animals here like those he encountered earlier. Something else was here, something they feared. As he got closer to the sparking, Terra saw it was a large vertical glowing bug light and it was attracting cannibal gnats to be electrocuted.

Below the light cage was a large stone bowl that was filled with crispy gnat bodies. Terra was amused by the sight at first until an orc stepped out from the forest, picked up a smaller bowl and dipped it into the larger one to gather some of the crispy gnats. He then started munching on them like popcorn. Not realizing it, Terra just stood there with his mouth open.

86. TERRA ENCOUNTERS FOUR DILOPHOSAURUS but has no fear of them knowing they sensed only a plant, not an animal.

87. **TERRA STOOD WITH HIS MOUTH OPEN** as he encountered an orc for the first time. **Upper Left:** The cannibal gnat.

"It was fantastic! Not only did Delos create an ecosystem of plants and animals but human-like creatures as well! Was this to be the future of life on Venus?" Terra thought. "Welcome to Mare Caverna" came a deep voice behind him. Terra turned around and looked up at the orc standing behind him. They loaded Terra into a wagon that was pulled by a dinosaur. He was taken across the forest to what looked like a primitive stone settlement. Terra was amazed by the number of orcs. He was also surprised by their general primitive living conditions. He knew somehow Delos created them and yet it was as though they had always lived in the caves of Venus far below the acid rain and heat above.

Terra was taken to a small room where they interrogated him. There he met the orc Rubin who identified himself as the chief administrator of Mare Caverna. After days of interrogation, Terra told them only that he was investigating the sudden appearance of cannibal gnats at the kelp settlements in the area. Terra was beaten and tortured. Fortunately for Terra, he was not the human he appeared to be.

Unable to get anything beyond what he told them, the orcs locked him into a small storage room. Stripped of most of his clothes, Terra laid on the dirt floor motionless and bleeding. He was in little danger from bleeding as his blood was more like sap. Still, the torture had taken its toll. Even though he had endured beyond what any human could, he was dying, and he knew it. Something was growing out of the palm of his right hand. It was like a small round seed pod. It contained all the memories of his life. As he laid in the dirt he realized his head, hands, and back rested directly on the soil of Venus. It suddenly occurred to him how strange it was that in all the time humans had been over and around Venus for the last 200 years, no one had placed their hands directly in the soil under cool safe conditions. Because of his plant side, Terra always felt a connection with soil. With only a brief direct touch he could tell what it was and what was in it. He had an almost a psychic connection with it. Almost at once he felt the soil here was very different from Earth. Terra wondered why he hadn't noticed it before.

Something was present in the soil here. The feeling jogged Terra's memory. He thought of the network of patterns in the first soil samples from Venus his predecessor examined years earlier back in 1903. He started to lose consciousness. Terra began to feel the presence of something. He felt he was not alone. There was something in the soil trying to communicate with him. In an effort to reach it he felt imaginary roots growing out of his back reaching deep down into the soil as he tried to make contact with it. Terra had a vision of himself lying in an alien field that had its own consciousness.

The ground was alive! In a further effort to reach the entity in the soil, he imagined more vines growing out of his body reaching out in all directions like a hungry plant trying to absorb all the nutrients it could from surrounding soil. The consciousness was a large collective of millions of voices coming from the ground all across the planet. Terra made contact. He learned millions of years ago Venus was once like Earth. When it started to heat up, some of its life moved into the soil. For both Terra and the entity, the contact was so alien it made any understanding of each other difficult at best. But in time it would become clear. As Terra's body died his consciousness moved into the soil. At the exact moment of death his right hand opened, and the round pod rolled out across the ground. The pod was like a large shiny white pearl. It would be another 32 years until the next Terra was born on Avalon Island.

In the hours that followed his death, Terra's body turned to solid stone. It was as though someone had created a perfect statue of his body in the final moments of his life. Later, after the statue was discovered by the orcs, Rubin ordered the room sealed. Just before leaving, he saw the pearl and reported it to Milton. Milton later had the pearl enclosed in a small medallion and wore it. The incident was not reported to Delos. Milton knew of Delos long time association with Terra. He did not want any attention drawn to the orcs or Mare Caverna.

88. **JUST BEFORE HE DIED,** George Terra had a vision of himself laying in an alien field that had its own consciousness. He was the first Terra to die before being able to surrender his memories to the next Terra.

As the years passed, news of the changing climate on Venus trickled back to Earth in a steady stream that few people paid attention to, that is except for some developers. When it seemed certain the land was indeed going to be habitable, some of them began to draw their plans. Since 1920 there had been land sale frauds on Venus. As a result, the "Bureau of Planetary Land" or "BPL" world organization was formed. It was an international organization located in Zurich, Switzerland. Since it was known the polar regions would become the first areas most likely for human habitation, they were of the most interest. One developer, however, multi-billionaire, Mac Sanders, had his eye on a different location in the northern hemisphere. It was a mountain outcrop in the middle of a vast flat plane. Sanders believed someday it would become an island surrounded by a warm ocean. He knew in all likeliness he would never live to see it, but his great grandchildren would if they kept the land in the family.

Sanders had filed a claim for the mountain outcrop back in 2020 plus a 500 miles radius extending out from the mountain in all directions. By 2045 the tricky part (especially for a claim on Venus) was the land had to be lived on for at least one Earth year. Even though conditions there were changing, it was still an average of 534°F [279°C] and 58 atmospheres. Sander's plan was to land at least one habitation module on the mountain and have a rotation of employees living there to represent his claim. Each shift was for a one-month period. Because Sanders had been an adventurer (before becoming a developer mogul) he decided to be among the crew of four that would take the first shift. When Sanders' claim was filed, it was brought to the attention of Delos. Because of his extensive activity on the surface of Venus, Delos made it a point to have someone on the inside of the BPL to report any claim that could be of possible interest or concern to his operations. Sander's name came up because his southern boundary was the northern border of Mare Caverna. Since Sanders' claim was beyond the outer boundary of Mare Caverna, Delos dismissed it as only a new distant neighbor to the north.

89. **MAC SANDERS** with two of his top employes working on Venus. **Left:** Dan Donnellson, hover falcon pilot. **Right:** Harry Hadley chief planetary surveyor.

On May 21st, 2046, the first habitation module with Sanders landed on the mountain outcrop that he now called New Seychelles (*SAY-SHELZ*). Although everyone that knew Sanders referred to the property as Sanders Mountain. Despite his dull surroundings Sanders was excited about making a move on Venus while his competition still considered it too dangerous. As the days passed, he felt the brown dreary atmosphere closing in. Part of their assignment was to go around the outer border and stake boundary markers. Sanders decided to divide the job among the first 4 crews. Each would journey to the outer boundary, stake out one quarter of the circumference and journey back. It would be 1785 mile [2872.7 kilometer] round trip. To make the trip, Sanders modified a hover falcon space craft. The hover falcon had been used successfully for years as a hybrid vehicle that flies like a helicopter in the atmosphere and its small internal drive engine enables it to fly in space. Sanders modification had the windows, skin, and all external features replaced with a heat resistant ceramic. To compensate for the increase in weight the internal drive engine was removed. As a point of safety, Sanders arranged to always have a floating station over New Seychelles, and it was always positioned within the hover falcon's range.

On the morning of the fourth day after their arrival Sanders, his pilot Donnellson, and surveyor Hadley lifted off from camp to lay the first boundary markers. Less than a day later they landed at the western border. Sanders was able to plant the first marker before night came. They could hear the roar of thunder from a storm. Over the next few days, they continued to plant boundary markers as they slowly headed around the first quarter of the border circumference. Sanders would be glad when it was over. Despite the slowly clearing atmosphere and slightly cooler temperatures, Venus was still a hellish place. The experience was like flying through a severe dust storm back on Earth, only here on Venus the ship's rotor turned at a lower speed because of the thick air and the storms seemed far more intense. Often after landing they had to wait for the storm to clear out for fear of being struck by lightning. It became clear to Sanders why none of his competitors had yet filed any land claim on Venus.

90. ON THE MORNING OF THE FORTH DAY Sanders and his team lifted off from camp to plant boundary markers.

At the very southern edge of the boundary there were more storms. As they approached the point where Sanders was to place the southernmost marker, powerful winds from the storms carried the ship to the south. Over the last few days, they had been struck by lightning several times, but this time it was far more intense. The ship's antenna was blown off completely. They could no longer make contact with the camp or anyone else. Donnellson could no longer keep the ship steady. As he tried a gain altitude the ship was struck by another volley of lightning. The ship started to lose power. One of the good things about the hover falcon was its ability to auto rotate like a helicopter. Donnellson turned to the south to get away from the storm as much as possible. Despite being able to make a soft landing, the ship still rocked back and forth as the storm passed by. Later during the night after the storm had passed, there was a violent earthquake. Looking out into the darkness Hadley thought he saw several large plumes of fire off in the distance. Since there was almost no oxygen on the surface, he was curious about what gas could fuel such a fire. The quake ended almost as quickly as it began.

At first light of the next day, Sanders, Donnellson, and Hadley began to assess their situation. Hadley was able to determine they landed 200 miles beyond the southern boundary. As Donnellson feared, engine failure was due to an electrical system that was shorted out during a lightning strike. It could be repaired but only with components from Hadley's navigation equipment. The repair would take two days. Hadley wasn't too concerned. One of the good things about Dana's rotation of the planet's core was the magnetic field it created made the use of a simple compass possible. Even though he hadn't used it in years he always carried one in his equipment.

As Sanders assisted Donnellson on the engine repair, Hadley decided to go out and explore the area, especially where the fire plumes were seen. As he got out, away from the ship, he could see the fire plums had come from an area just beyond an outcrop of rock less than a mile away. As he made his way over the rocks he looked down at the large open chasm before him. It was almost like looking down into a miniature Grand

Canyon. After a closer inspection he could see the break was recent, probably caused by last night's quake. Looking down from the edge, Hadley could see that the roof of a grand cave below had collapsed. He surmised when flammable gas in the cave was exposed to the 500°F+ [260°C+] atmosphere above, it triggered the explosive fire plumes he saw the night before.

Hadley couldn't explain the fine ash powder all around. And there was something else. All around there were patches of what was first thought to be fine white gravel with tiny sharp points. But after a closer look Hadley remembered where he had seen this before. It wasn't gravel at all. It was bone fragment, the same kind found after cremation. Hadley collected a small sample, but the surrounding heat of Venus' atmosphere made it almost impossible. He also surmised the dark ash power all around was not from something inorganic. "Before the cavern roof collapsed, there was something alive down there, but what?" Hadley thought to himself.

It was a calm morning on the third day. Because of some delays in making repairs, they didn't lift off until mid-morning. Looking back thru the lower aft cabin window, Hadley tried to get a glimpse of the chasm from the air but could see very little due to the constant poor visibility of the Venusian atmosphere. Looking out, Hadley thought he saw something flying in the air just beyond the chasm. It looked big and dark and was coming in their general direction. At first it was like a twisting dark form inside a bubble. He pulled away and rubbed his eyes. When he looked up again it was gone. Hadley dismissed it as his imagination as he came away from window. Right now, he had a more important job, guiding Donnellson back to place the last boundary marker and then back to the camp.

Later after placing the last boundary marker, they lifted off. After what they had been through, they were all looking forward to getting back. As the hover falcon gained altitude the visibility got a little better and rays of sunlight broke through some of the dense brown, yellow clouds all around. To Donnellson it felt good. He knew once back at camp it would be unlikely that anything like this trip would happen again until his tour of duty was up. Suddenly the ship was in another shadow. It struck Donnellson funny because the clouds above were broken yet the shadow was constant.

He looked up and a wave of terror came over him. Above was a gigantic, winged creature flying inside of some kind of bubble. After a moment he could see it was some sort of dragon. It started to plunge down towered them. Donnellson turned the ship into a quick dive shouting. "Something out there is diving at us! Strap yourselves in!"

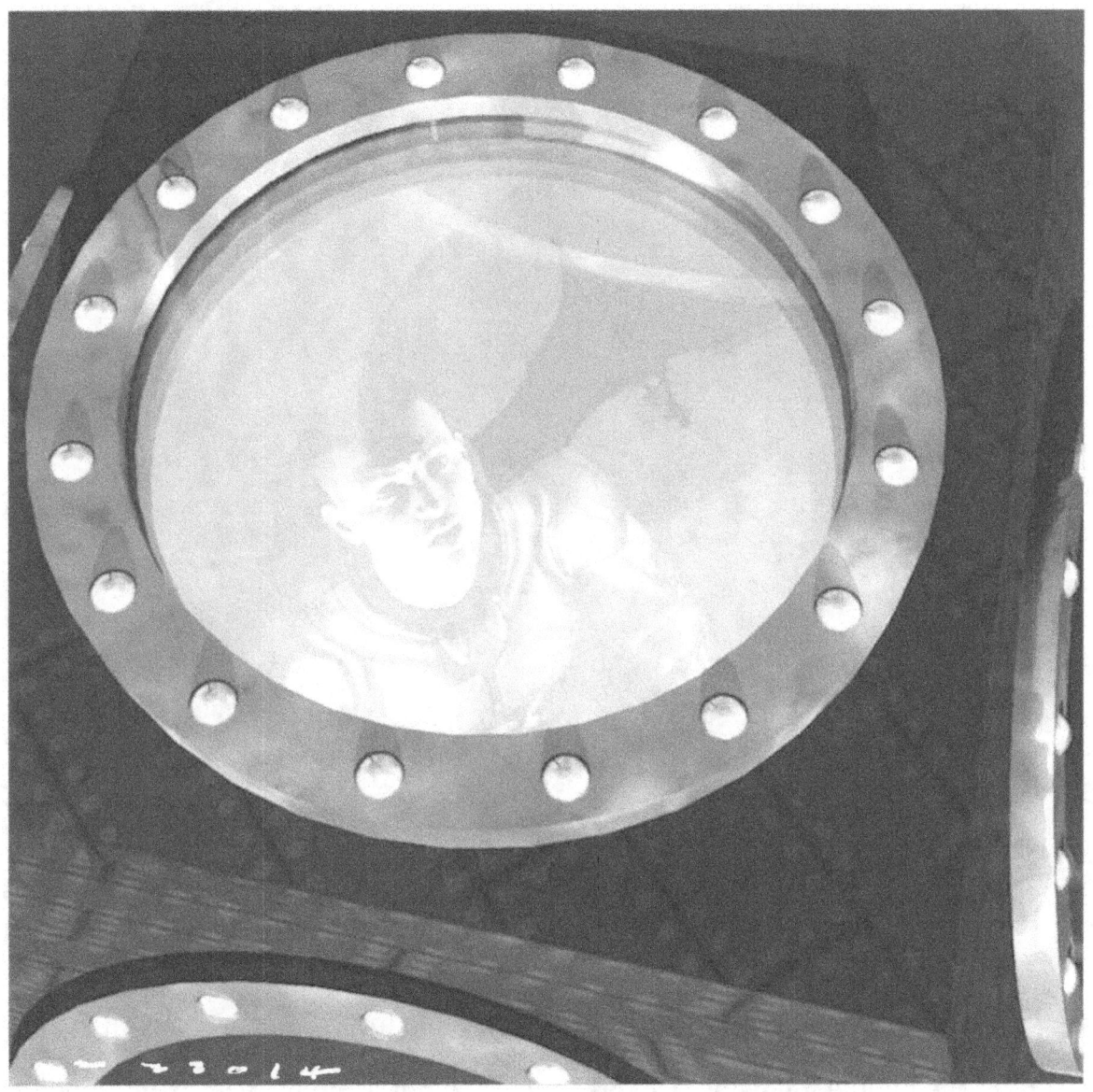

91. AS DONNELLSON LOOKED UP; a wave of terror came over him. Above was a gigantic, winged creature flying inside of some kind of bubble.

92. HADLEY GOT TO THE BACK WINDOW with a camara. He could see the creature in the bubble following. He did his best to put aside his fear as he filmed the beast.

It suddenly lunged forward into a power dive. With its claws extended it tried to pierce the upper hull of the falcon. As it tried to tear away at the ship's outer skin the creature cried out as though it was getting burned by touching the ship. It pulled away cutting into the ships rudder as it went. Hadley kept filming. Now flying behind the ship, the creature began to fold its wings again to gain speed. It was flying much lower this time and looked like someone was riding on it! The air was thick, and it was too far away to get a good look. Without warning a piece of the rudder came off and flew directly back, hitting the creatures back, striking the rider and something just behind him. Suddenly the bubble collapsed, and the creature burst into flames and was gone in an instant. As Hadley continued to film, the creature's bones broke up into small fiery chunks as the hot air of Venus consumed it completely.

With part of the rudder broken off, the ship was becoming unstable. The hover falcon was starting to spin around in circles. "Suit up any way you can!" Donnellson shouted. With the g-forces acting on the ship, Hadley knew he would never make it. He rushed to pack the camera in its ceramic case. A few minutes later the hover falcon crashed, the hull breached and in an instant was consumed by the heat of the outside air. Sanders was the only one to survive. Donnellson and Hadley were killed instantly. Most of the ship was quickly reduced to smoldering ash. Sanders pulled out one of the rescue cases. It contained a harness and inflatable ceramic balloon with a rescue beacon. On Venus balloons were commonplace. Long ago it was determined plucking a rescue victim from a balloon 40 miles [64.4 kilometers] up was much easier than getting them out of a blast furnace. Within an hour Sanders was well on his way to the upper atmosphere where he was picked up six hours later.

93. **THE ONLY SURVIVER, MAC SANDERS** dangles from a rescue balloon as he ascends 40 miles [64.4 kilometers] up from the hover falcon wreckage.

Mac Sanders returned to camp days later to finish his shift. He wrote a journal of the events prior to crashing but kept the dragon sightings quiet fearing he might be labeled as an unstable person, especially when he had no hard proof of what actually happened. Six months later back on Earth, Sanders was approached by Silas Marnier who requested a private meeting. Marnier was a low-level analyst with Planet Watch. After the "Venus Event" (when the planet was bombarded with SEE energy to shorten its day) it also created many seismic disturbances. The Planet Watch organization was created to monitor any on-going surface activity. Since that time, Planet Watch has monitored the planet using what they called a secondary imaging system.

Marnier explained if there is any surface activity the primary imaging system focuses on the area producing highly detailed pictures. Such was the case of the disturbance where Sanders reported his forced landing. Marnier said the primary imaging system was still operating long after the surface event ended. He admitted he would have ignored the finding completely except that the system indicated the "unusual activity detected" sign. He reported Sander's hover falcon vanished then reappeared on the system before it crashed. Also, just after reappearing, for a brief instant, there was another image of what looked like a large bird on fire that was following the hover falcon. Then it was gone. Marnier showed Sanders a poor image of the event.

Upon seeing the image Sanders decided to tell the whole story of what actually happened. He also mentioned that one of the crewmen, Hadley, said something about protecting his camara before the ship crashed. Sanders also remembered Hadley said he collected some unusual bone dust samples when they had to land the first time.

Marnier wanted Sanders to accompany him to the crash site, but Sanders had no interest in returning.

94. **THE PLANET WATCH IMAGE** that started the investigation.

On March 3rd, 2047, Delos received a request from Marnier of Planet Watch to conduct a close-up inspection of the disturbance that took place on the northern border of his property near the Stratus floating settlement. Marnier indicated the inspection was for geological study only and made no mention of the images or Mac Sanders. Delos had no objection, but the request aroused his curiosity. He wondered if it was related to the quake that rocked the northern part of Mare Caverna nine months earlier. Delos informed Milton and asked him to visit Rubin to inform him of the Planet Watch request and see if there was any possible danger of being discovered. Upon his visit to Mare Caverna on March 14th Milton was surprised how much things had changed. He learned Rubin had been conducting his own regeneration experiments and, in the process, created a miniature underground ecosystem of dinosaurs like those at Elysium Donte. What Milton didn't know was that in the process, Rubin created dragons and was able to fly them using protective TLA fields. Milton was shocked and wondered how Rubin had managed to keep all of it a secret. Then Rubin went into detail how the dragons had been trained by orc riders and eventually replaced the pluto airships to patrol the area around Mare Caverna. Milton realized that Rubin had his own liaison with Dr. Serco, and it was Serco who had provided the dragons or the means to create them in the first place. It was clear that Rubin no longer considered himself under Milton. Upon seeing all that had changed, Milton quietly began to fear for his life.

Rubin had proclaimed himself the ruler of Mar Caverna. Upon hearing the news of Planet Watch coming, Rubin wondered if the site inspection of Planet Watch had anything to do with one of his dragon patrols that went missing while investigating a geologic disturbance. Rubin sent the patrol because the collapsed cavern had been under development. Not long after Rubin was given charge over Mare Caverna, both he and Milton began a secret program seeking out other places to develop protected ecosystems. That was 32 years ago. By now there were several separate underground chasms, all miles apart from each other, and aside from Milton, only a few of his most trusted orcs knew the locations of all of them. Rubin remembered after the first patrol dragon disappeared other patrols were sent into the area but didn't find anything. The quake destroyed one of the smaller ecosystems, but the heat and pressure of the atmosphere above removed any evidence of its existence. In the interest of staying hidden from humans a little longer, Rubin decided not to send any patrols into the area while the Planet Watch expedition was there.

Fearing for his life, Milton showed only admiration for all Rubin had accomplished. Rubin announced Mare Caverna was breaking away from any outside authority or control and offered Milton a high position in his military. Milton agreed with the idea of breaking away from human control but stated the time had not yet come for any action. Rubin thanked Milton for the warning of Planet Watch coming and allowed him to leave.

95. RUBIN GAVE THE ORDER TO KILL MILTON shortly after his airship departed Mar Caverna.

When Milton's airship was out of visual range from Mare Caverna, he turned the ship east. He knew the bubble surrounding his airship would prevent any detection. Unconvinced of Milton's loyalty, Rubin gave the order to attack his airship after he departed. Shortly after Milton's departure, Rubin started his attack on Stratus by severing all its anchor cables from the ground. At that same moment, a group of dragons and their orc riders flew out of a deep abyss several miles away. Like a stream of underwater bubbles, they flew up into the yellow clouds.

Aside from the loss of communications, there was no immediate sensation at Stratus after the cables were cut. Then the city slowly began to drift with the wind. Minutes later the dragons came out of the clouds near Stratus and attacked. Everyone on Stratus was horrified by what was happening. With nothing to stop them, the dragons descended and tore into the balloons of Stratus. There were also several explosions during the attack. After the first dragon was sighted, the attack was over in just 17 minutes. No longer buoyant, Stratus began to break apart and list over on its side. When the last balloon was torn open, the settlement with 2000 human personnel plunged down into the clouds and was gone. It was almost 32 years ago to the day that Stratus was first established. Because there was no seismic activity in the area at the time, the event wasn't observed by Planet Watch. Rubin watched from an observation window to see the returning dragons. He faintly smiled as the distant rumble of Stratus crashing miles away could be heard and felt slightly. The dragons pursuing Milton never found him and returned.

96. SURPRISE ATTACK! Without warning, the creatures came out of the clouds all around. At first the inhabitants of Stratus couldn't believe their eyes. Then suddenly their amazement turned to shock as they had no time to react to the horror that was suddenly upon them.

Upon receiving news of Stratus, Delos was furious. He also wondered about Mare Caverna. Now there was no direct surface communication. Stratus had been the only means of direct contact with Rubin. Five days later Milton arrived at Elysium Donte with more detailed news of Rubin's activities and intentions. It was clear to Delos the existence of the orcs on Venus would soon be known to the outside world. At last count, two years ago back in 2045, Mare Caverna had an orc population of 30,000. "What a waste" Delos thought.

Three days later a lone pilotless aircraft descended into the clouds over Mare Caverna. At 20 miles [32.2 kilometers] up it fired a single rocket that exploded on the surface two minutes later. The blast destroyed the roof of Mare Caverna's central cavern. The intense heat and atmospheric pressure incinerated Caverna City. Less than a minute later the craft flew down into the crater opening and exploded deep inside the underground cavern network. The explosion was equivalent to a medium uranium bomb. Because its superheated shock wave was somewhat restricted and channeled by the underground cavities, over 90% of its force penetrated as far as 100 miles in all directions. The disturbance created a series of aftershocks that extended out as far as 200 miles. The event was so great it was picked up by Planet Watch. As Delos looked out over the cloud tops from his chamber he was saddened by the loss of his investment. Checking his pocket time piece, he looked at Milton and quietly said "It's over".

Delos later explained the loss of Mare Caverna was due to volatile refinement materials that were breached when Stratus crashed down from above. Up in the northern part of Mare Caverna territory, the Planet Watch expedition led by Silas Marnier landed and began the search for Sander's wreckage. Marnier knew the odds of finding anything were very remote. Like the bottom of Earth's oceans, the surface atmosphere on Venus was subject to currents and they could have easily scattered the wreckage for many miles. After an extensive search Marnier found only a few small fragments of the craft.

Milton wanted an independent life for the orcs, but after what happened on Mare Caverna it was clear Delos was still in charge. After the incident, Delos began to have second thoughts about creating the orcs. They clearly demonstrated their work ability but if word ever got out that they were his creation, it could prove fatal for him and his organization. Delos had the idea of terminating the orcs when Venus became cool enough for human settlement but was uncertain when the best time would be. On July 10th, 2052, that decision was made for him when Elysium Donte was destroyed in a massive quake. There were no survivors. All but one of the pluto airships was accounted for. Delos assumed Milton had been incinerated with the others.

97. **THE GREAT QUAKE OF 2052** all but destroyed Elysium Donte. It triggered a chain reaction that caused the tankless atmospheres to collapse one by one.

98. WITH THE COLLAPSE OF ALL ELYSIUM DONTE'S tankless atmospheres the population (even those wearing protective working gear) was incinerated in an instant. A section of the dome covering the main entrance to the mines gave way, allowing the heat and pressure of the outside air to enter the tunnels below. In a strange twist of fate, all the pressure doors were open at the time.

151

The years passed. Delos decided to rebuild Elysium Donte, but only with mechanical workers and human personnel. Now that tankless atmospheres had become common place, he no longer had to keep the site as restricted like before. By 2060 it was up and running again. The surface temperature of Venus was now down to just over 481°F [249°C] and surface pressure at the lowest elevation was 54 atmospheres. Many of the settlements that had cropped up in the green patches of furnace kelp became abandoned as the kelp became less buoyant in the now thinner and cooler atmosphere. With the decline of sulfuric acid in the atmosphere, their tankless atmospheres were being deactivated. All over Venus the taller kelp started to collapse. The kelp roots remained anchored firmly into the ground, penetrating miles deep. The average height of surviving kelp was now 40 miles [64.4 kilometers]. Because of the danger from falling kelp, tight building restrictions were in place until it could be determined if the planet was safe.

In 2073, George Powers Terra the 2nd (7th) woke up in the greenhouse on Avalon Island. He was born with only the memories of his predecessor Paul Powers Terra (5th) who surrendered his memories 50 years earlier back in 2023. In the days that followed, George Terra tried to learn more details about why there was a break in the Terra line. He surmised George the 1st had been killed and as a result 50 years was missing from his memory. According to his journal, dated 32 years earlier on January 5th, 2041, George the 1st was leaving for Venus to investigate the appearance of cannibal gnats on furnace kelp that was in two specific regions. Terra decided to continue the investigation of his predecessor. While reviewing history, he learned the region of interest was a location where the floating city of Stratus had been destroyed back in 2047. Shortly thereafter, a grand cataclysmic event on the surface below created a vast canyon feature that extended for miles outward in all directions.

99. **2073, GEORGE POWERS TERRA** (the seventh of his kind) is born in the greenhouse on Avalon Island. He is missing 50 years of memory because his predecessor was unable to return and surrender his memories.

After learning all he could from his predecessor's journal, Terra returned to Venus to investigate further. The area of interest was where the city of Strata had been destroyed. Since the area was still under the control of Delos, Terra decided to visit him first. In early 2074 he arrived at Delos City. Terra's last visit with Delos was 43 years ago in 2031. The last Delos heard of Terra was when he was investigating a cannibal gnat infestation back in 2040. There had been no word from Terra since. A long passage of time without seeing someone was not unusual for anyone in the immortal's club. Delos knew Terra would often go into hiding for years on end. During their meeting, Terra did his best not to reveal that the last 50 years of his memory was missing. He asked for permission to investigate the Stratus site. The reason he gave was to investigate the possibility that the ground explosions that followed Strata's destruction may have been caused by underground gases produced by the deep roots of furnace kelp. Delos knew furnace kelp's existence was to alter gases on a planetary scale and was not surprised by Terra's request. He gave his consent for Terra to investigate the site.

Terra's airship arrived at the general Strata site five days later. During his travel, he sighted several large furnace kelp balloon clusters that had broken off as the atmosphere of Venus became thinner. They were clearly a dangerous menace to navigation. Upon reaching the site where Strata once was, Terra's airship slowly descended into the dark orange clouds below. The area was now almost completely devoid of any living furnace kelp. Like the remains of a gigantic ancient forest, the broken sections of kelp were all around. As he got lower, he saw even more remains of kelp nearby had been blown out in all directions. On the surface directly below was a miniature Grand Canyon with tributaries that stretched out in all directions. Like his predecessor, Terra believed the presence of cannibal gnats meant the possibility of an enclosed area that was growing lunar mushrooms may have existed at one time. A warning light came on. His sensors detected the harmful rays left over from the uranium bomb. "Whatever was here, someone went to a lot of trouble to cover it up", he thought to himself. Beyond uranium detection, the immediate area didn't reveal anything unusual.

100. BY 2074 THE BROKEN BALLOON CLUSTERS of furnace kelp had become a dangerous menace to navigation on Venus.

As Terra's airship circled over the magnificent canyons below, he wondered if the site might become a tourist attraction on a terraformed Venus in the future. Before leaving the surface, he decided to follow one of the larger tributaries to see how far it ran and for any clues on what might have been here before. He began heading north. As he got further north, the chasm below began to narrow. Surface bridges crossing over the gorge began to appear. Terra decided to see how far the gorge ran. He set the ship down for the night and resumed in the morning. As he traveled further and further the bridges eventually became caves that were open at both ends. It confirmed Terra's theory that the entire canyon system or at least a large part of it had been a grand network of caves at one time. Further on, the gorge became a series of smaller gorges.

Several days had passed. It was getting dark again. He had traveled just over 900 miles [1448.4 kilometers]. Off to the left there was an outcrop of rock. Terra decided to pass over it before leaving the surface. As he got closer something shiny caught his eye. It was twisted metal of some kind. He landed nearby. Terra got out to get a closer look. The site was clearly the wreckage from something. Typically, on Venus very little of any kind of wreckage survived for very long. As Terra looked around, he could see that it was the remains of a hover falcon. Sifting through the wreckage he discovered several ceramic cases. He was very careful not to cause any further damage as he retrieved them. Among them was Hadley's camera case. After 28 years of exposure to the intense heat and pressure of Venus' atmosphere, the ceramic camera case had sealed itself completely. Terra decided not to cut it open until he was safely away.

The spying eyes were everywhere on Venus. Terra felt it was best to secure what he collected and not examine it until he was back on Earth. Two weeks later, on Avalon Island, Terra examined the images from Hadley's camera and saw the dragon flying in a tankless atmosphere. It was the first hard evidence that backed up stories of creature sightings that had been circulating on Venus for years.

101. AFTER 28 YEARS, TERRA DISCOVERED the lost wreckage of Mac Sanders hover falcon.

Until now, Terra gave little thought to the stories of flying monsters on Venus. He believed they were simply an extension of the UFO stories back on Earth. As he examined the artificial bubble enclosure that was protecting the dragon, he realized it was the result of the material stolen from the Tower of Venus 150 years ago back in 1924. Terra surmised the flying creature was most likely an artificial creation that resulted from the use of lunar mushrooms. Dana's tankless atmosphere had been reversed engineered into a portable version to protect it against the harsh conditions on Venus. He knew Delos or someone working for Delos was behind it. Whoever it was, they were probably the same ones who murdered his predecessor when he started investigating.

After the frightening discovery, Terra invited Marriana Dana (4th) to visit Gilgamesh Island. When she received the invitation, Dana was some puzzled because her time for regeneration wasn't to be for another six years in 2080. As it was for most immortals, many years had passed since their last meeting. The first moments of their meeting were the exchange of pleasantries over years since last seeing each other. Terra expected Dana to have changed, but there was something more, something much more. Dana spoke of other worlds that were many light years away. She not only knew of them but had been there. It was clear to Terra that she had firsthand knowledge of the universe that humanity wouldn't know of for many centuries to come. Dana revealed her pursuit of interdimensional physics led to the discovery of gateways that allowed her to travel to other parts of the universe in real time. Being somewhat overwhelmed, Terra sat quietly for a moment as he processed what she had just told him. He also realized he might be the only person she trusted with that knowledge.

All Terra had to offer was the fact that the last 50 years of his past were missing. He revealed to her that he had re-engineered the regeneration process, so the body of his predecessor was no longer required beyond surrendering his memories. Terra suddenly realized Dana was the only living person he trusted even though any meeting or correspondence was years apart.

He showed her the images from Hadley's camara. She had been informed of the Venus Tower robbery years earlier, but Terra didn't think they had stolen enough to be of any use. While curious about the scale of an operation that could produce these creatures and protect them, Dana decided they posed a threat to anyone who was going to settle on Venus after the planet was terraformed.

After looking at the images of the dragon again, Dana suggested the dragons might not be the result of regeneration manipulation, but they could have been brought in from a distant world. Someone else may have discovered gateway technology. Dana had firsthand knowledge of a world that had dragons.

There was no question the flying dragons had to be eradicated and the best way to do that was remove their protection from the Venusian atmosphere by neutralizing their tankless atmospheres. The surface temperature was now approximately 462°F [238°C]. That would be hot enough to finish the job. Dana told Terra the tankless atmospheres could be disabled, but the energy pulse that does it requires line-of-sight. She also said it was most likely these creatures are from a protected underground area that might be difficult or impossible to find. There was no assurance of neutralizing all of them.

When Terra asked for clarification on disabling the tankless atmospheres, she further explained the kind of energy pulse required. The pulse itself is harmless to people but would render the artificial element of Veridium3 nonconductive. Veridium3 was a metallic ceramic that was composed of tube-like structures so small they could only be seen through an electron microscope. Their electromagnetic properties made a new kind of micro electric power possible in the smallest of circuits. Because of its high production costs, it wasn't widely used. She showed an image of it on a small monitor she carried. The image stirred up a memory from Terra's distant past.

Later, out of curiosity Terra looked at Veridium3 images. They reminded him of something, it was a sample of ore he had examined many years earlier, but he couldn't remember exactly were. For days he tried to jog his memory until it came to him. Yes- he remembered now, it was back in late 1902, 172 years and several life segments ago when he saw a similar pattern in some soil samples brought back from Venus.

In 2075, unknown to anyone, several pilotless aircraft descended from space and began flying under cloud cover to patrol areas on Venus where stories of flying creatures originated from. They became engaged in a secret war, a war that took place just out of view from the floating settlements above. There were many engagements between the aircraft and flying dragons. In most cases the dragons burst into flames as the bubbles protecting them collapsed, but it was not without losses. The cost of the war weighed heavily on Terra's resources. Over the course of his life spans he'd acquired many land and financial holdings. To finance the war, he sold off a chain of islands in the south pacific. He took the blame for the tankless atmosphere falling into the wrong hands. Terra thought, "If only I had concealed the temperature and pressure gages when showing the furnace kelp to Delos for the first time. Had he done so, Delos never would have known of the tankless atmosphere's existence in the first place".

In 2080 Delos came to Gilgamesh Island to regenerate. Delos had no knowledge of Terra's death at Mare Caverna, and he also wasn't aware that Terra had direct knowledge that artificial creatures had been created on Venus. Terra was careful to conceal the fact that he was investigating Delos and wondered if Delos knew he was behind the attacks on dragons. The regeneration went as normal, except this time Terra had arranged a small diversion releasing hundreds of small birds in the lab making it appear like they had broken a window. During the chaos Terra swapped out the skull from Delos left over skeleton. It worked. Once Delos was away, Terra pulled Delos former skull out of hiding and started his examination.

102. **"THE SECRET WAR"** as it was later called, broke out on Venus, and was fought almost entirely in the air under the veil of thick cloud cover. During the 15 years the encounters lasted, 257 attack drones were lost and an estimated 196 dragons were incinerated. Because the drones had to have line-of-sight to deactivate the dragon's tankless atmosphere the dragons, who were faster and more maneuverable proved extremely difficult to kill.

After being regenerated, Delos returned to Venus. Unknown to anyone, he had a private chamber where he housed his collections. Most of them were bones collected from prisoner regeneration experiments that had gone wrong. Also among them were the skulls left over from his previous lives. As he was about to place his most recent one on its pedestal there was something about it that wasn't quite right. It felt a little heavy. He carefully compared it to an earlier one. They were almost a perfect match. Delos realized Terra had switched skulls. He became furious and threw the fake against the wall. It shattered into pieces on impact. He knew sooner or later Terra would discover his true identity, Abraxas Delos. His first thought was to have Terra killed immediately. A moment later as his anger cooled, Delos thought it best to think the matter through until he could decide what the best time and circumstance would be. He knew Terra had many powerful friends.

Even though Terra's real home was Avalon Island in the frozen Antarctic, he still maintained labs on Eden Island. The Tower of Venus was still in use, but now it was being used to simulate the atmospheres of other planets and moons. It wasn't long until Terra discovered that the skull retrieved from the regeneration of Delos was not that of Alexander Delos. He soon discovered it was that of Abraxas Delos, although Terra found it hard to believe it at first. Terra knew Abraxas Delos was the adopted son of Alexander Delos. Abraxas was thought to have been killed in an accident 185 years ago, back in 1895, but didn't die. Instead, he murdered his father and assumed his identity. Terra remembered choosing Delos to join the immortals club because of all he had accomplished throughout the solar system. That was in 1880. He remembered Delos changed in the years that followed. As Terra thought further, he knew it was unlikely that the Delos he remembered from the early years would ever joined the Shadows.

103. **DELOS WAS FURIOUS** when he discovered the skull he was holding wasn't from his previous body.

Delos received word that there was unexplained drone activity in the region around Mare Caverna. He wondered if someone was investigating the site for the way it was destroyed. Before dealing with Terra, he decided to investigate the matter. Several days later his airship was in the area. As he flew around, he saw no sign of unusual activity. He decided to have his ship fly around in an outward spiral to see if anything was happening around the outer perimeter. He also activated the ship's tankless atmosphere to avoid any possible detection. Days passed. Since his arrival his airship had traveled several thousand miles. Still flying on a steady course around the central area, he was now 700 miles [1127 kilometers] from the center of Mare Caverna.

His pilot spotted something off in the distant horizon ahead. It looked like a furnace kelp balloon cluster that had broken off. With the atmosphere cooling there were so many. The problem was the ship's sensors indicated nothing was there. Why would that be? As Delos looked through his telescope, he could barely make out the faint blue bubble all around it. The balloon cluster, or whatever it was, had concealed its presence using a tankless atmosphere. Delos had the ship keep its distance and drop down into the clouds. He made his way to the crow's nest at the very top of the ship then gave an order to climb until he was just high enough to see the balloon cluster again. As he looked out using his telescope. He saw two balloons open like flower petals and release small flying objects. They were drones of some kind. That balloon cluster wasn't a cluster at all. It was a disguised base ship. But what was it for and what was it doing out here? Delos thought to himself.

Delos decided to drop further below the clouds and follow the drones. As they departed from their base, they became visible to the ship's sensors. Delos's airship descended deeper into the clouds. The drones were descending to a lower altitude and out running the ship. Delos tried to follow as best he could. Soon he was at a much lower altitude. Only his tankless atmosphere kept his airship from burning up. There was no way he could keep up. Delos tried to keep them in sensor range as long as possible. He fell so far behind that he was about to give up pursuit when the drones stopped flying on a straight course and begun to fly like gnats around a light.

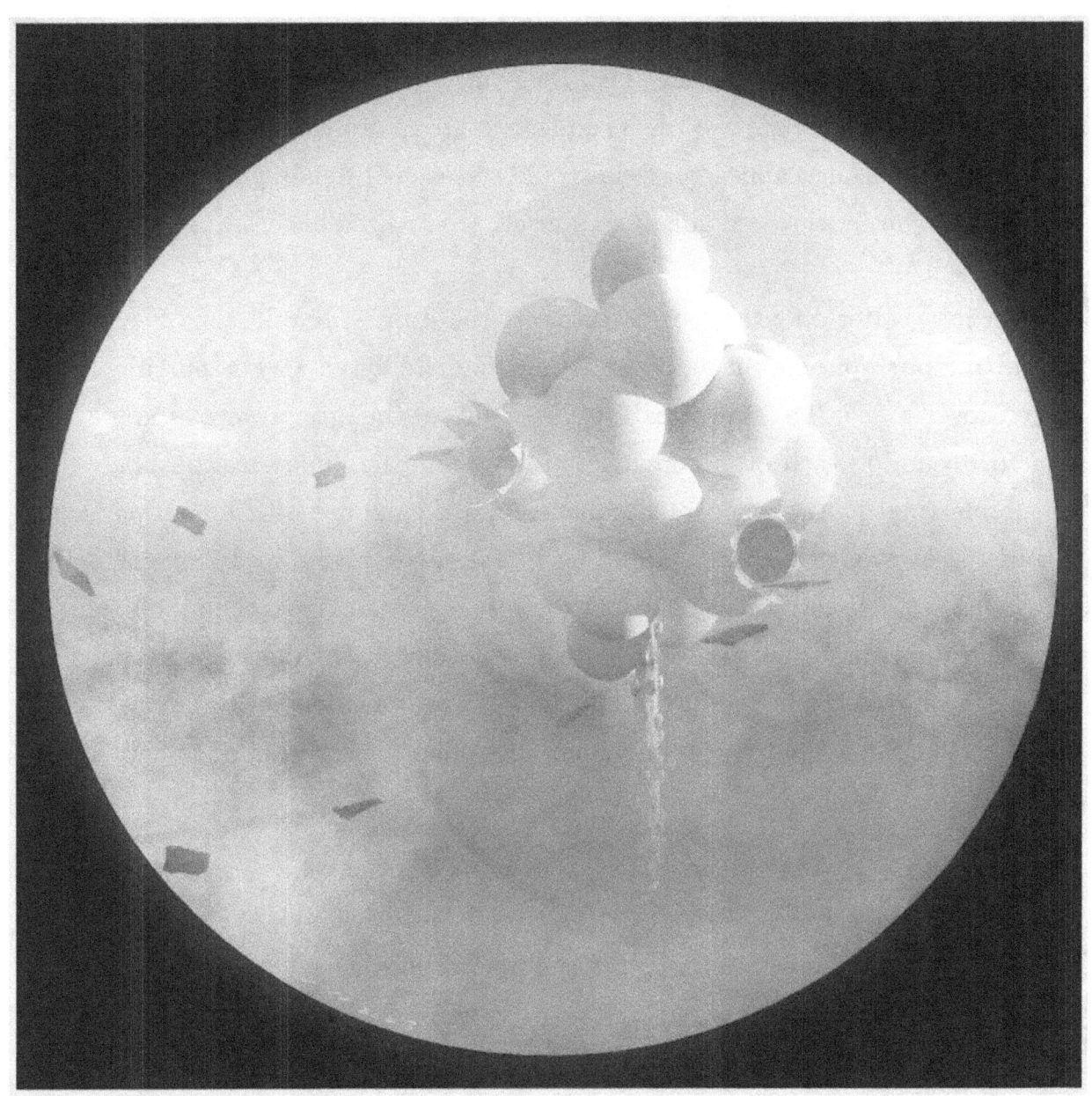

104. LOOKING THROUGH HIS TELESCOPE, Delos could see that the furnace kelp balloon cluster wasn't a cluster at all, but rather a hidden base of some kind. What was it for? What was it doing out here? Delos thought to himself.

Delos wondered what was going on at first then it suddenly occurred to him that the drones were engaged in some sort of air battle. As he watched his sensors, the flurry of activity slowly began moving in his direction. Then they broke into flying straight toward his airship and were closing fast. Delos maneuvered the ship to get out of the way of the approaching drones, when suddenly a group of flying dragons appeared. A second later the drones appeared. Delos could see each of the dragons had orc riders. "Rubin's Dragons" Delos said quietly to himself. He realized his uranium bomb didn't destroy them all.

To get in a better offensive position against the drones, the dragons began to fly around the airship, using it as cover. The drones followed in hot pursuit. As the dragons tried to tear the drones apart, Delos could see the drones were trying to focus a narrow beam on each of the dragons. As they did, the tankless atmospheres that were protecting the dragons would collapse and they along with their rider would burn up. Even though the dragons and drones seemed only interested in each other, Delos knew he was in terrible danger. If he lost his tankless atmosphere his airship would burn up. He started to ascend as fast as he could. The fighting continued and both sides still showed no interest in the airship. It was as though the airship was like a large rock in the middle of a ground battle, as both armies continued to fight around him.

The air battle started to move away from his ship. As he feared, it suddenly happened. A beam from one of the drones took out his tankless atmosphere. The ship's hull started to burn. Running the engines at full, Delos desperately tried climb to cooler altitudes. The outside was getting cooler, but not fast enough. The engines had heat damage and were beginning to fail. Delos was so busy he didn't notice the ship's sensors detected two vehicles approaching from above. The engines stopped and the airship slowly started to descend into the fiery inferno below. Since first coming to Venus Delos knew there was a possibility of being burned up alive, but until now he never thought it would actually happen.

105. **AS THE AIR BATTLE CONTINUED,** the dragons and drones seemed only interested in each other. Despite that, Delos knew he was in terrible danger and started to ascend to cooler altitudes.

Delos could hear faint noises coming from above. Something was happening on the ship's upper hull. Cables were being attached to the upper hull's frame. Before Delos could react, the ship started to ascend once more. He went to the crow's nest to see what was happening. Two cables had been attached to the ship. Each was suspended from a hover falcon. Delos's ship was being ferried back to the floating base he saw earlier where the drones originated from. Upon reaching the base, the hover falcons lifted the airship above the base where he and his crew could depart from the gondola safely. After that, they flew off and released the airship. As they did so, the empty airship slowly descended into the clouds and was gone.

Delos was surprised, even a little shocked to see Terra. He suddenly realized a secret war was being fought between Rubin's dragons and Terra. It was obvious to Delos that Terra knew about Rubin's dragons, but he wondered if Terra knew anything about the orcs. In an effort to hide his association with the orcs, Delos reported after Mare Caverna and Stratus had been attacked, he dropped a uranium bomb in an effort to eradicate them completely. Delos said he came back to investigate the rumors that dragons had been seen again. Terra appeared to believe his story. He told Delos of the break-in on Eden Island years ago and the dragons and whoever is behind them are using the stolen technology to protect the dragons and themselves from the atmosphere of Venus. Terra was hoping to recover what had been stolen by destroying them completely if possible. Delos offered his help. Terra accepted and from that point on their alliance turned the tide of the conflict in their favor. It was an uneasy alliance. Although they were cordial to each other, Terra wasn't sure who he was dealing with. He decided to go along at least for now until the dragons had been eliminated. Delos had similar thoughts. He felt the discovery of a possible link between him, and the orcs was more of a threat than Terra discovering his true identity.

106. HOVER FALCONS SAVE AIRSHIP long enough for the crew to be safely offloaded.

By 2090, the pilotless patrol craft no longer encountered any dragons. Both Terra and Delos continued to search the land using ground penetrating sensors but turned up nothing. Because the surface temperature was now down to 385°F [196°C] and the pressure was now 42 atmospheres the dragons no longer burst into flames like they did when the conflict started, they simply fell to the surface and baked. To prevent further discovery, Delos had their bodies stripped and burned.

By this time Terra, Delos and Dana had conformation that a sub-humanoid race had also been created. Delos, of course, pretended to know nothing. Many years later when news of the secret war came out in the open, it became known as "Iron War I". Elysium Donte was now 187 years old since the time it was founded as a mining site back in 1903. With lower temperatures, the rate of mechanical worker loss was greatly reduced. Small temperature fortified surface settlements begin popping up in the polar areas on Venus where the temperatures would be the lowest as the planet continued to cool.

Having a hand in their creation, Delos knew about the sub-human race of orcs. What he didn't know was both Milton and Rubin had survived what happened at Elysium Donte and Mar Carvana. Rubin knew Mare Carvana would be destroyed after the attack on Stratus. Prior to the attack he had moved a considerable force to Mar Regoon, an underground cave network almost the size of Mar Caverna. When the quake struck Elysium Donte, Milton was at Mare Tuskan, another underground cave network. Both sites were the two largest secret caverns known only to orcs. They were located near the equator and had orc populations in excess of 10,000.

Back on Eden Island (Earth) the sun was setting, and a full moon was rising in the east. Terra finished transmitting the latest entry in his journal. Now that the dragons were gone Terra knew he would have to eliminate Delos. He felt Abraxas was a murderer who had no right to the immortality that had been granted to his father. In the moonlit clouds above, a single drone enclosed in its own faint blue bubble, quietly descended over the island. Just as Terra was about to close his journal, something out of the greenhouse window caught his eye. As he looked up, he could barely make out a small black dot falling out of the clouds. As it fell, it turned toward the island. Realizing what it might be Terra turned to run toward the vault door to open it.

There was a bright light behind Terra. It blinded him. Less than a second later a powerful shock wave blew out the greenhouse windows. He was blown across the room slamming into the wall. Before he could get to his feet, a high wall of fire roared across the island, destroying everything in its path. It all happened so fast. There was no time to react. In the brief remaining seconds of his life, he could only watch as everything was instantly consumed in fire. From a distance, the mushroom cloud could clearly be seen as it consumed Eden Island. Back on Venus, Delos received confirmation of the strike and that Terra was on the island at the time. "It's over", he said quietly to himself, as he looked out over the yellow cloud tops.

107. IT'S OVER, Delos said quietly to himself, as he received word that Eden Island had was obliterated and Terra was on the island at the time.

When news of Terra's death reached Dana, she was deeply saddened, then she became furious. Unlike most bombs, uranium bombs leave a distinct signature. After a short time, she learned the uranium used came from a deposit near Elysium Donte. It confirmed her suspicions of Delos. Dana had enemies in the past. They were all gone, but she never killed any, at least not directly. Instead, she sent each of them to live out the remainder of their lives in their own private hell. She felt the best punishment was to send them to a world where they would be forced to face the worst part of themselves and there was no way out.

After a brief look into Delos's history, Dana learned of the hundreds of mechanical workers that burned up during the early days of Elysium Donte, and the fate of prisoners who were also there. Unknown to most, Dana was the most traveled person alive. Years ago, during her experiments in interdimensional physics, she discovered places the rest of humanity wouldn't learn of for centuries. She knew of a place that was inhabited by living machines who were not friendly. Dana knew once Delos was there, the remainder of his life would likely be similar to his mechanical workers. Dana was very patient. She knew Terra had a vested interest in seeing Venus terraformed and Delos might still be of use until that goal was reached. She decided she would wait for now. Later, when the time was right, the doorway to that other world would come for Delos and there would be no way to escape from it.

The years passed. Venus continued to cool. Dana arrived on Avalon Island in 2123, 33 years after Terra had been murdered on Eden Island. Terra's biological and mechanical defenses took no action against her. She knew the time had come for him to be born in the greenhouse. Standing on the upstairs balcony of his grand manner, she looked across the blue lagoon at the greenhouse nestled in the deep foliage beyond.

108. **NANCY DANA** (6th) arrived at Avalon Island in 2123 to be there when Terra would emerge from the greenhouse. It had been the second time he was murdered before he was able to return to the greenhouse to surrender his memories to the new body. When Terra emerged, he became Henry Powers Terra (the 8th of his kind). Dana revealed the information she had on George Terra (7th) prior to his death on Eden Island.

After Dana revealed to Terra everything she knew of his resent history, he decided to visit what was left of Eden Island. He knew the vault on the island could resist a uranium bomb if its door was closed. Wearing protective clothing, both Terra and Dana went to Eden Island by means of the gateway she had invented.

109. EDEN ISLAND had been completely decimated by the uranium bomb. Fortunately for Terra, the vault door was closed, and he was able the retrieve the journal from his predecessor.

Terra decided the best thing to do was not to act on Delos until the terraforming of Venus was complete. He also urged Dana to do the same. Terra also suggested to Dana that she should consider changing her regeneration process to be the same as his. If anything should happen to her, another one would rise to continue on, just as he has. She agreed. When the time came for her to regenerate in 2130, she had already established a remote greenhouse on an earthlike moon many light years away. It was also the year for Delos to regenerate. After the murder of his predecessor, Terra assumed Delos had already made his own arrangements to regenerate. Terra decided the best thing to do for now is to let Delos think he had succeeded in his murder. Terra wondered if any of Delos' shadow associates also had a hand in his murder.

In 2140 as the temperature dropped just below 213°F [101°C] the first hot steamy water areas began to form on Venus. Many of the surface settlements along the shores edge became known as steam towns. At first it was thought, with the changing conditions on Venus, they would only last a short while, like the kelp settlements. But for many, life in the steam towns developed a hearty culture all their own and as the planet cooled, they slowly migrated south from the polar regains. In an interesting twist of lifestyle, they had large aquariums that were filled with Maine lobster (from Earth) and the heated steamy oceans provided the power that kept the aquariums cool. When it was time to eat, the lobsters were dipped in the Venusian oceans to boil. It was said they had a wonderful taste that was unlike any other. So much so that steam town lobsters attracted tourists visiting from off-world.

110. **THE STEAMTOWN OF NEW FRESNO** began as a floating settlement in 2163. By then the temperature of Venus was down to 166°F [74°C] and 25 Atmospheres. As Venus cooled and water levels rose, the city simply floated to the nearest coastline. New Fresno was one of the few steam towns that later developed onto a major city. In 2173, Henry Powers Terra regenerated and became Oliver Powers Terra (the 9th of his kind).

111. IN 2183 A DEADLY LIFE FORM was introduced to the warm waters of Venus in the narrow shipping lane of the Corono Sea by Dr. Serco. At first a bubble with Dr. Serco formed underwater. Seconds later, another bubble formed. It was a gateway to the warm waters of another world. Almost at once, deadly alien fish began to appear as they swam through the gate. Their skin was like iron, and they could chew through wood and metal. Reports of missing ships began to circulate soon after their arrival. Dr. Serco enjoyed introducing alien life forms to an unsuspecting population. He was amused by the death and chaos it would create.

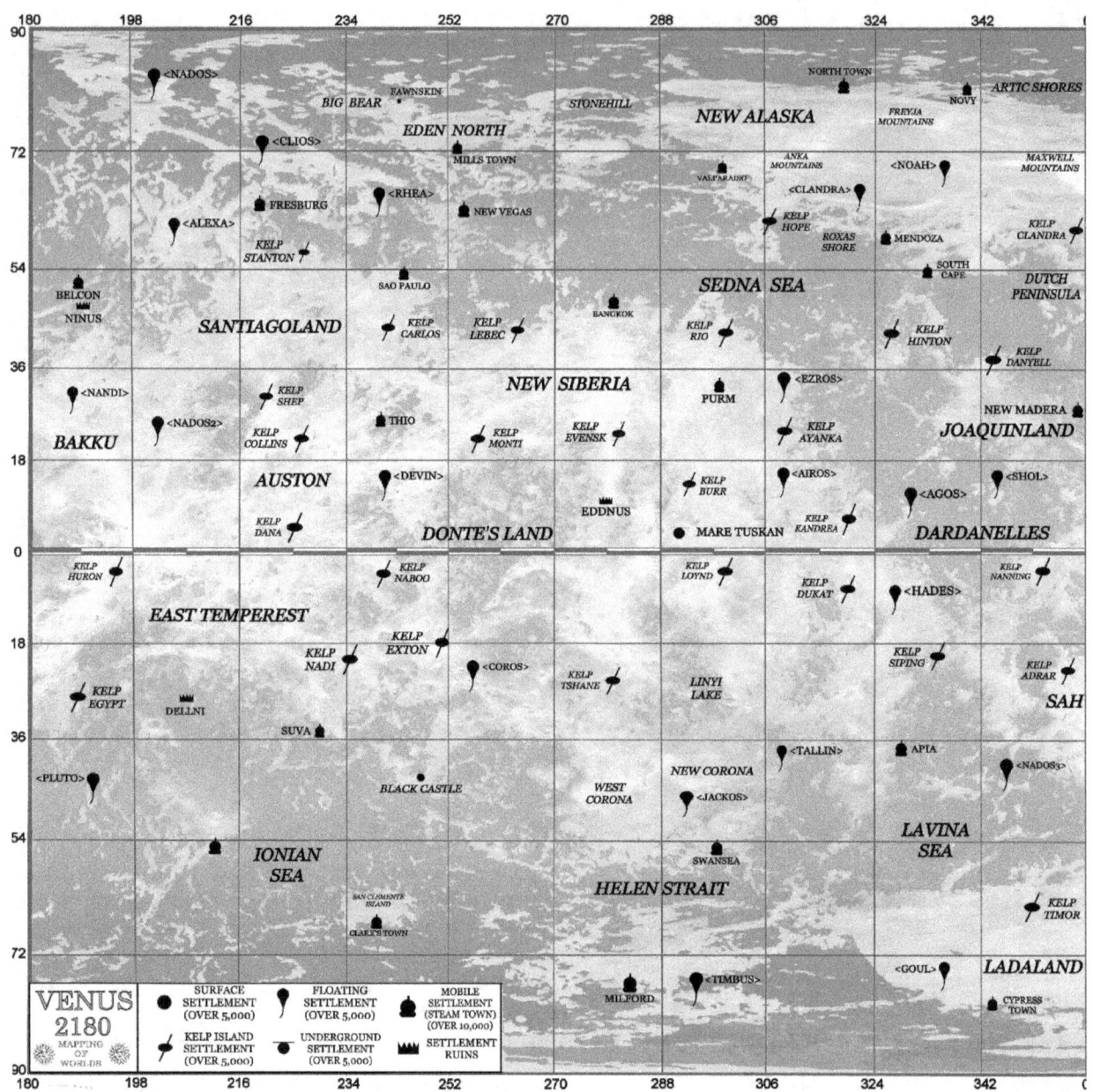

112. BY 2180 THE CONTINENTS OF VENUS were becoming distinct as the planet continued to cool. The average surface temperature had dropped to 133°F [56°C] and pressure was down to 20 Atmospheres. The air was becoming breathable to the orcs. Concealed by the constant cover of the cloud belt and tankless atmospheres, they began to come out into the open. (land image by NASA)

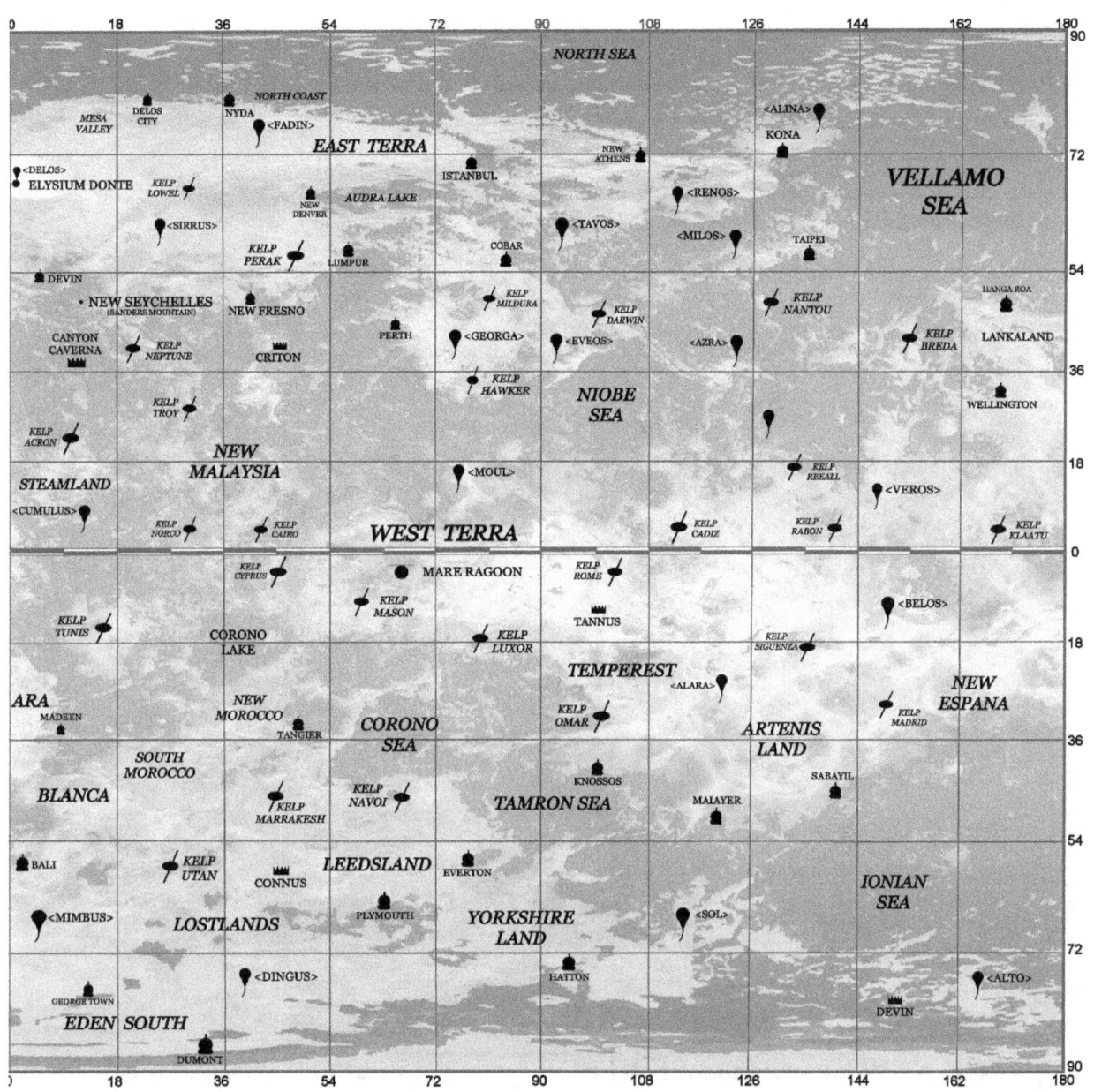

113. **THE NEW SEYCHELLES RESORT** opened in 2190. What had once been a mountain in a hell hole was now in the early stages of becoming a vacation place. Markus Sanders was a direct descendant of Mac Sanders who first founded the property 170 years ago, back in 2020. The average surface temperature was now 119°F [48°C]. The resort was kept to a cool 72°F [22°C] under the tankless atmosphere. Note: Fake ruins were constructed nearby. Sanders had them built to attract divers after the sea levels rose.

114. **THE LIFE CYCLE OF FURNACE KELP** ended with the rise of cities made mostly from fallen kelp. The only living kelp remaining was a smaller version in the cloud belt. Oliver Powers Terra (9th) was pleased to see that the life cycle of furnace kelp went as planned. In 2223, he regenerated and became Ronald Powers Terra (the 10th of his kind).

115. **THE CLOUD BELT** is the only area that did not become earthlike after Venus was terraformed. With temperatures averaging 161°F [72°C] the belt remains the hottest place on the planet. It extends 500 miles [805 kilometers] each way from the equator. Travel across the belt is best done by high altitude air or by submersible (other than the Corono Sea).

116. **WHAT WAS ONCE ELYSIUM DONTE** was now a high-altitude, pressurized weather station. The former mining city came to an end in 2183 when a devastating quake destroyed the site. What began as a site for mining nearly 365 years ago at the doorstep of hell itself, the site of Elysium Donte was now dominated by the ruins of its past.

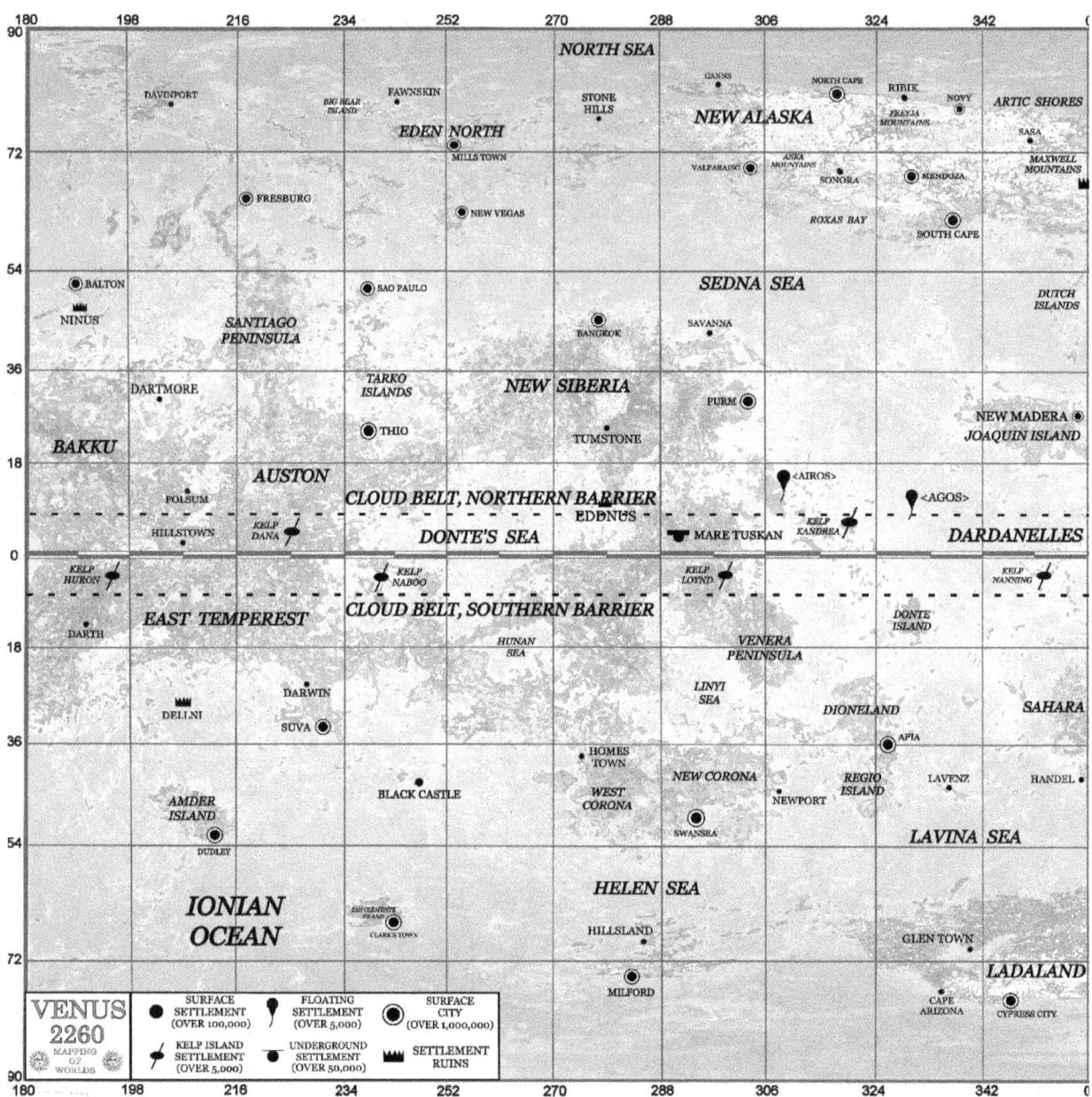

117. BY 2260 THE PLANET VENUS was considered fully terraformed or at least as much as it could be given its proximity to the Sun. The average surface temperature at sea level in the polar regions was now 76°F [24°C]. That meant the northern and southern hemispheres would be somewhat isolated from each other because of the hot cloud belt on the equator.

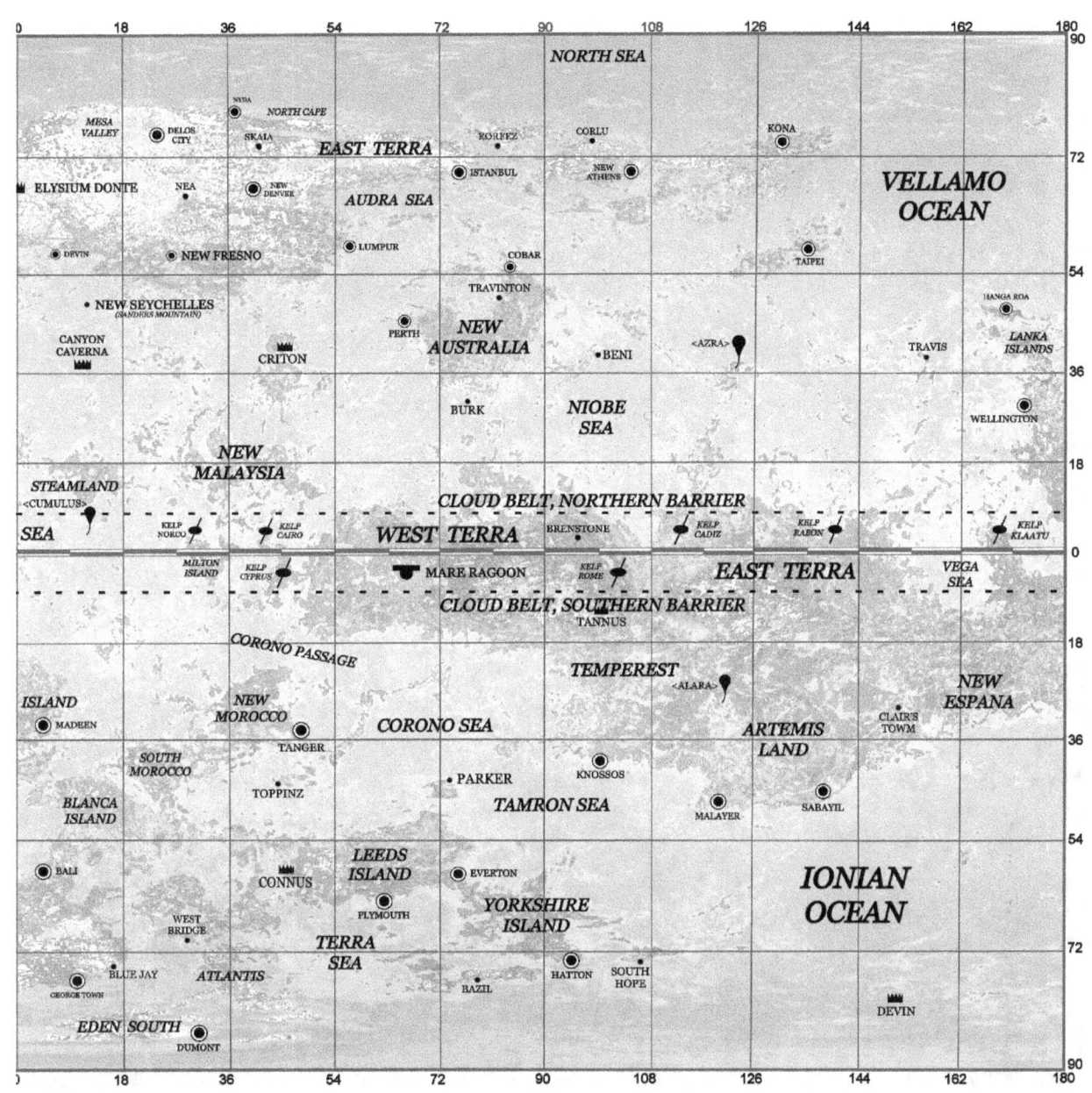

[SURFACE IMAGE: Is a combination of NASA, 1Wyrmshadow1, and Tim Dooley. The artwork of "1Wyrmshadow1" can be found online at deviantart.com.]

118. **THE DREAM OF MAX SANDERS** finally came to pass in 2260. Dana Sanders, the first granddaughter of Markus Sanders became the chief administrator of the island resort. New Seychelles (Sanders Mountain) was directly between two major cities, making it a highly successful stop over place.

119. THE VIEW OF AN EARTHLY VENUS from the Venera space station was a site many had waited years for. The terraforming of Venus was considered complete, at least to Delos and his associates. The Venera space station was becoming to Venus what Ellis Island was to America in an earlier time. The average global surface temperature was down to 87°F [31°C] and pressure was at one atmosphere.

The Shadows had replicas of the Black Castle throughout the solar system. The one on Venus was built in a remote area in the southern hemisphere. Less than a month after it was finished the entire site including all occupants and even the grounds was turned to stone.

120. **THE GROUND IS ALIVE!** That was the last message received from the newly established Black Castle on Venus. Then all communication went silent. Dr. Serco was the first on the scene. After staying only for a few minutes, he returned to Earth and advised no shadow member (except Delos) to set foot in Venus. Serco felt Delos was expendable now that Venus was terraformed. He also felt that Delos was becoming too well-known and might draw unwanted attention to the Shadows. While he was there, Serco noticed a curious stone bust of Terra on the building cornerstone.

Near the North Pole, the planned city of Stone Hills was the first major surface city to be established. It was the creation of off world developer Albert Hill. Located near the north pole, Stone Hills consisted of a series of grand towers that were built on the high points of a ridge that became islands as the North Sea formed.

The year was 2261. Venus was Terraformed. Dana decided the time for Delos was up. Delos (now the 9th of his kind) had a penthouse that had a commanding view of the city. He profited from the development of Stone Hills, and it was just the beginning. "In the years to come I'll be the richest man in the solar system" he thought to himself. He left the women he was with on the balcony and went to the back of the penthouse. A moment later in the bathroom he heard a strange noise coming from the hallway. It was like the sound of a crackling wood campfire. He stepped and stood in the hallway. At the other end was a vertical cloud of energy. Delos was terrified. He didn't know what it was and stumbled back as it started to move toward him. The hallway was the only way out from where he was. Delos jumped across the hallway into another bedroom. As the energy cloud came closer, he continued to stumble backward until he was against the wall. The apartment's power went out. Looking through the doorway, he saw blue light from the cloud's lightning growing brighter as it approached. He covered his eyes as it entered the room. A moment later it was upon him.

The noise stopped and the power came back on. Still horrified the woman he was with slowly came back in off the balcony. The interior was in shambles, like the aftermath of a powerful storm. Now there was only silence, as she called his name and slowly made her way to the bedrooms. The cloud left a burn trail on the floor. Entering the room where Delos had been, a black outline where he stood against the wall was all that remained.

121. DELOS WAS LAST SEEN in the city of Stone Hills. In 2261 Delos vanished in a blaze of light and was never seen again anywhere in the solar system.

122. AFTER DELOS VANISHED, he wasn't killed or disintegrated as everyone thought. Instead, Delos had been pulled through an interdimensional doorway that led to a planet 16 light years away. It was in a double planet system in the 4th orbit around its star. It was a dry, cloud covered planet with breathable air. It was also a planet of hostile living machines. Before Delos could react, they were upon him.

In 2273, the cool twilight sky hung low over the ice peaks of a small uncharted island off the coast of Antarctica. Cold, gentle waves of a quiet tranquil sea lapped gently against the icy shores of Avalon. The island's interior continued to be the warm valley oasis teaming with life Terra had established 365 years ago, back in 1908. Ronald Powers Terra (the 10th of his kind) went to the greenhouse to surrender his memories. Laying down flat, he positioned his head into an open flower and fell into a deep sleep before passing on. After sitting quietly for 50 years in the greenhouse the large pod slowly opened revealing the next Terra. As he adjusted to direct exposure to air and light for the first time, Alfred Powers Terra (the 11th of his kind) stood up.

The doorway to Venus was open. As expected, the early years of the twenty-fourth century saw a grand migration to Venus. It was almost a second Earth. The new world would bring great opportunities for a new life. For most, the greatest of which was to live free from the shadow of big government back on Earth (at least for a while). A new age for human expansion was coming. But the new Venusians would not be alone because the planet had already been exposed to human folly and sooner or later humanity would have to face it as history once again repeats itself.

There was something else. Two powerful sub-human nations were concealed in the cloud belt. Dr. Serco delighted in the uncertain outcome it would bring.

123. **THE STORY OF VENUS** is far from over-

The **Illustrated Tales From An Alternate Steampunk History** series is based on a collection of stories that were posted online over a period of several years. These stories cover the lives of characters, both good and evil, human, and non-human, natural or created, and some that live between the centuries. Throughout the timeline their lives and actions set off a chain reaction of events that create an extraordinary woven pattern of history that spans from the time of ancient periods to the centuries that lay ahead. The series is not limited to Earth or Human history, but also covers non-human, off-world events, some of which had an influence on humanity. Because of my interest in Steampunk, several stories take place in the 19th century where: genetic engineering, terraforming, and faster than light drive have become a reality with unexpected treasures and consequences.

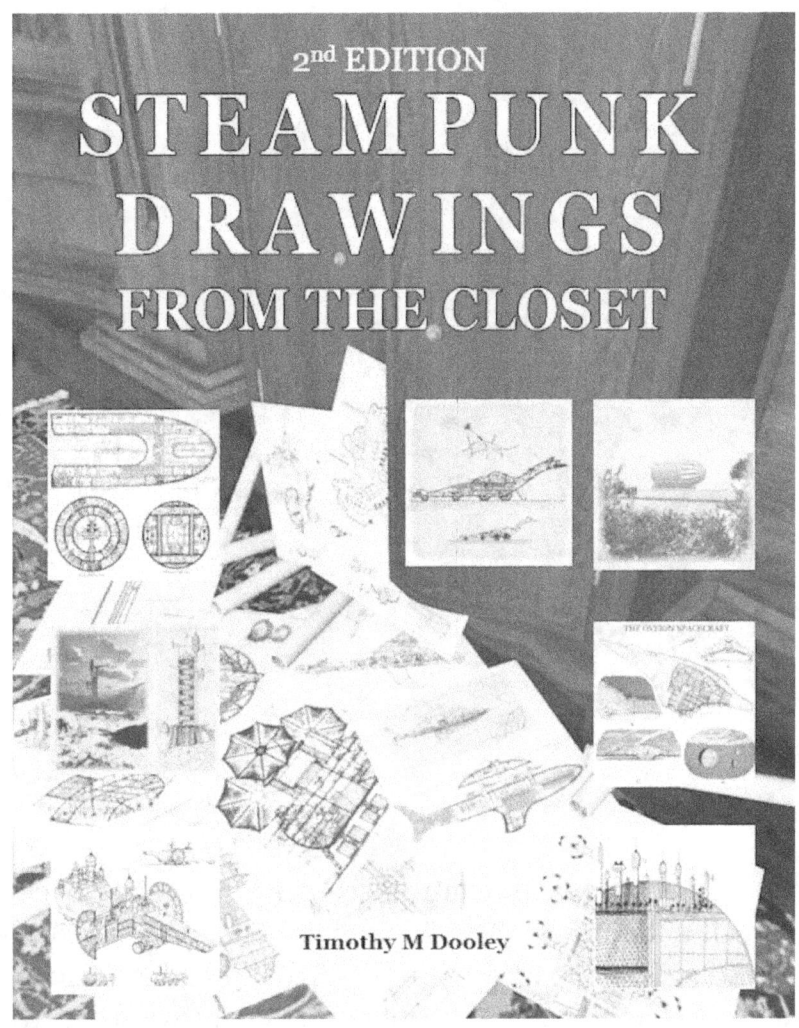

Steampunk Drawings From The Closet is a book for anyone who has an interest in the general design of ships, aircraft, land craft, spacecraft, and cities that one might find in the world of 19th century science fiction. As long as I can remember I've had a deep fascination with the world described by Jules Verne and H.G. Wells and many other authors of that period. My longing to see further into that world motivated me to create many technical drawings and illustrations. Most of them have been buried in my closet for the past 40 years and have not seen the light of day. Recently, there has been a voice telling me I need to get them out into the open (while I still can). I am the only one who knows about them and the story behind each drawing. To all who long for the world of Steampunk, it is my sincere hope that you will enjoy them as much as I enjoy sharing them with you.

Tim Dooley's interest in 19th century science fiction goes back to the late 1950's after seeing the movie "The Fabulous World of Jules Verne". During the 70's and 80's, He illustrated fantasy machines that included airships, land steamers, flying machines, submarine steamships, off-world cities, planetary and interstellar spacecraft. In 1986 these drawings created an opportunity for him to work as a Designer in the aerospace industry. In 1994 His drawings caught the attention of the woman who later became his wife. In 1997, one of the airship drawings he did was published in the Orange County Register's Focus on Science page. In 2003, he started creating scratch-built models of my own design for what he called "The Jules Verne Room". Over the years he posted illustrated stories all of which were based on an alternate timeline. At the suggestion of others, he is now in the process of converting those stories into semi-graphic books.